SCIENTISTS AND THEIR DISCOVERIES
ISAAC NEWTON

SCIENTISTS AND THEIR DISCOVERIES

ALBERT EINSTEIN

ALEXANDER FLEMING

ALFRED NOBEL

BENJAMIN FRANKLIN

CHARLES DARWIN

GALILEO

GREGOR MENDEL

ISAAC NEWTON

LEONARDO DA VINCI

LOUIS PASTEUR

THOMAS EDISON

SCIENTISTS AND THEIR DISCOVERIES
ISAAC NEWTON

PAUL M. NITTANY

MASON CREST

Mason Crest
450 Parkway Drive, Suite D
Broomall, Pennsylvania 19008
(866) MCP-BOOK (toll-free)
www.masoncrest.com

Copyright © 2019 by Mason Crest, an imprint of National Highlights, Inc.

All rights reserved. No part of this publication may be reproduced or transmitted in any form or by any means, electronic or mechanical, including photocopying, recording, taping, or any information storage and retrieval system, without permission from the publisher.

Printed and bound in the United States of America.

CPSIA Compliance Information: Batch #SG2018.
For further information, contact Mason Crest at 1-866-MCP-Book.

First printing
9 8 7 6 5 4 3 2 1

Library of Congress Cataloging-in-Publication Data

ISBN: 978-1-4222-4031-1 (hc)
ISBN: 978-1-4222-7763-8 (ebook)

Scientists and their Discoveries series ISBN: 978-1-4222-4023-6

Developed and Produced by National Highlights Inc.
Interior and cover design: Yolanda Van Cooten
Production: Michelle Luke

QR CODES AND LINKS TO THIRD-PARTY CONTENT

You may gain access to certain third-party content ("Third-Party Sites") by scanning and using the QR Codes that appear in this publication (the "QR Codes"). We do not operate or control in any respect any information, products, or services on such Third-Party Sites linked to by us via the QR Codes included in this publication, and we assume no responsibility for any materials you may access using the QR Codes. Your use of the QR Codes may be subject to terms, limitations, or restrictions set forth in the applicable terms of use or otherwise established by the owners of the Third-Party Sites. Our linking to such Third-Party Sites via the QR Codes does not imply an endorsement or sponsorship of such Third-Party Sites or the information, products, or services offered on or through the Third-Party Sites, nor does it imply an endorsement or sponsorship of this publication by the owners of such Third-Party Sites.

Publisher's Note: Websites listed in this book were active at the time of publication. The publisher is not responsible for websites that have changed their address or discontinued operation since the date of publication. The publisher reviews and updates the websites each time the book is reprinted.

CONTENTS

CHAPTER 1	Newton's Early Years	7
CHAPTER 2	The Teachings of Aristotle	17
CHAPTER 3	The "New Science"	31
CHAPTER 4	Light and Color	45
CHAPTER 5	Gravity and the Laws of Motion	59
CHAPTER 6	A Very Eminent Citizen	77
	Chronology	86
	Further Reading	89
	Internet Resources	90
	Series Glossary of Key Terms	91
	Index	93
	About the Author	96

KEY ICONS TO LOOK FOR:

Words to understand: These words with their easy-to-understand definitions will increase the reader's understanding of the text while building vocabulary skills.

Sidebars: This boxed material within the main text allows readers to build knowledge, gain insights, explore possibilities, and broaden their perspectives by weaving together additional information to provide realistic and holistic perspectives.

Educational Videos: Readers can view videos by scanning our QR codes, providing them with additional educational content to supplement the text. Examples include news coverage, moments in history, speeches, iconic sports moments and much more!

Text-dependent questions: These questions send the reader back to the text for more careful attention to the evidence presented there.

Research projects: Readers are pointed toward areas of further inquiry connected to each chapter. Suggestions are provided for projects that encourage deeper research and analysis.

Series glossary of key terms: This back-of-the book glossary contains terminology used throughout this series. Words found here increase the reader's ability to read and comprehend higher-level books and articles in this field.

A London street scene during the Great Plague. Houses "visited" by the Plague were marked by a cross, and charcoal, pitch and brimstone were burned outside in the hope that this would kill it off.

WORDS TO UNDERSTAND

alchemy—the art and science that aimed at the "perfection" of matter through chemical operations understood in religious terms. The alchemist who could turn a base metal into gold was also supposed to have attained religious self-perfection.

apothecary—the ancestor of our druggist or pharmaceutical chemist. He prepared and sold drugs for medicinal purposes.

calculus—the mathematical method used to calculate the rate of change of continuously varying quantities by treating the infinitesimal differences between consecutive values of such quantities. There are two forms of calculus, differential and integral.

gravitation—Newton's Law of Universal Gravitation states that every particle of matter in the universe attracts every other with a force that varies directly as their masses and inversely as the square of the distance between them.

CHAPTER 1
Newton's Early Years

By the fall of 1665, the Great Plague of London was at its peak. Over 7,000 bodies were being thrown into mass graves every week. The Plague began to spread into the area east of London, including the university town of Cambridge. The colleges in Cambridge were ordered to close, and soon emptied of students and teachers. At night the town was bathed in the glow of fires of charcoal, tar, and brimstone, which were kept burning in hopes that they would kill the "poison" of the Plague.

Among those forced to seek refuge in the countryside was a young scholar from Trinity College named Isaac Newton. He went to his mother's farm at Woolsthorpe in Lincolnshire. Except for short visits to Cambridge, Newton spent nearly two years there. His teachers at the college had believed Newton showed great promise as a scholar. But they could not have guessed what he was to discover in those two years, shut away most of the time in a lonely village. Newton made some of history's greatest scientific discoveries. His work was to give a firm basis to a new kind of science, that replaced the ancient structure of knowledge that had stood for two thousand years.

One of Newton's discoveries was that white light was really made up of rays of different colors. Another was his method of "fluxions," or **calculus**, as it is now known, which is a very powerful mathematical tool. The third, and perhaps the greatest, was to lead to the Law of Universal **Gravitation** that ruled the fall of an apple to the Earth as well as the motions of the planets around the sun.

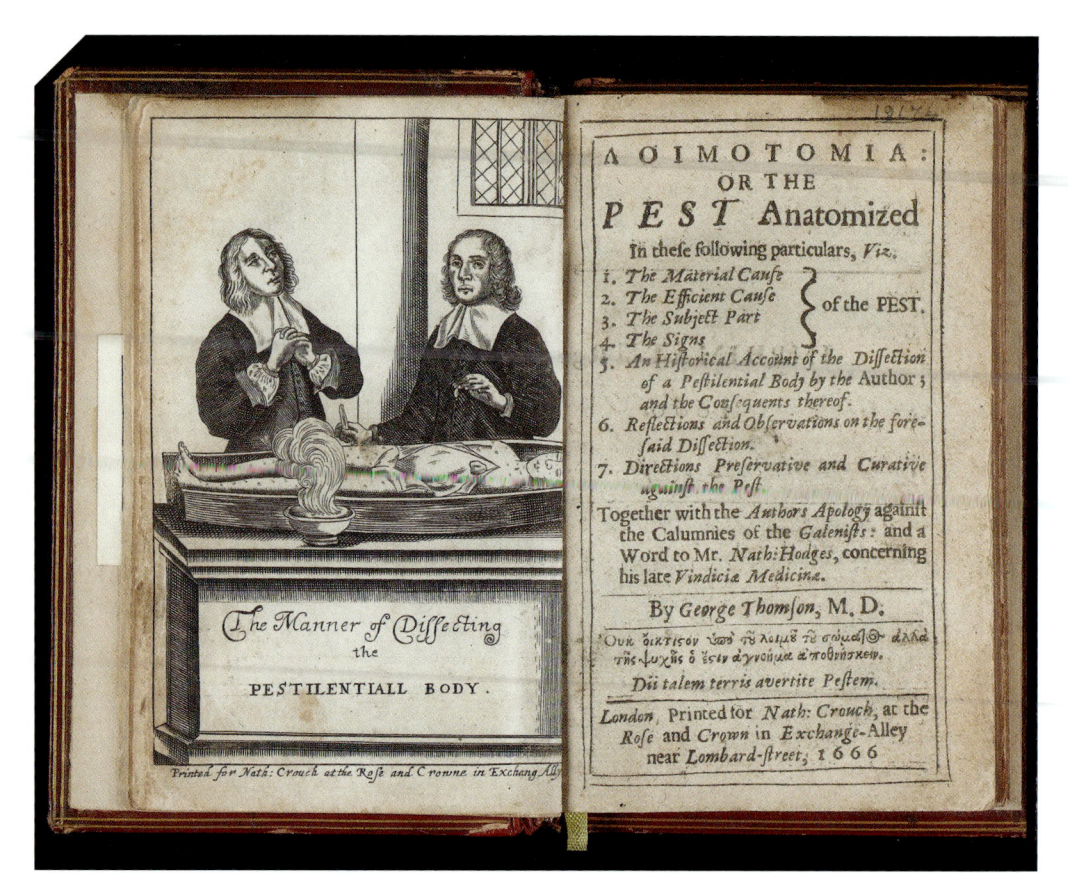

Two men dissect a body covered with Plague marks in this illustration from a medical book about the London Plague. Incense is burning in a nearby bowl to camouflage the stench of the body. More than 100,000 people died during the Great Plague of 1665.

To grasp Isaac Newton's true greatness, a modern student must try to understand what science was like in the seventeenth century, before Netwon's discoveries changed it forever. That is one of the hardest, but the most valuable, rewards of traveling through history. Newton did not work on scientific problems only, but also spent a great deal of time studying Biblical prophecy and **alchemy**. Strange pursuits indeed for one of the founders of modern science! But for Newton, his scientific work was just one aspect of his search for an understanding of God's great plan as it was revealed in nature and in history.

Birth and Childhood

Isaac Newton was born on Christmas Day, 1642, at the small manor of Woolsthorpe, about six miles south of Grantham in Lincolnshire, England. He was the son of Robert, a farmer, and his wife Harriet. Robert had died only a few months after his marriage and three months before Isaac's birth. Born prematurely, Isaac was said to have been so small that he could have been put into a quart mug. He was so weak that two women sent to fetch medicine for him did not expect to find him alive on their return.

When Isaac was three, his mother married the Reverend Barnabas Smith, a well-to-do rector, and went to live in the nearby village of North Witham. Isaac remained at Woolsthorpe, where his grandparents raised him and began his education.

Isaac Newton's birthplace at Woolsthorpe, a small village near Grantham in Lincolnshire, England

The free school at Grantham, founded by King Henry VI, where Newton was educated as a boy.

Newton attended two little day schools, and went to the King's School of Grantham when he was about twelve, lodging at the house of an **apothecary**. A seventeenth-century writer described him as a "sober, silent, and thinking lad," who was set apart from his school-fellows by his precocity and inventiveness. He made some remarkable mechanical toys and models, such as a windmill, a waterclock, and a carriage moved by the operation of a handle by the person who sat in it. He studied how paper kites could be made to fly higher and be more maneuverable. The paper lanterns he attached to them frightened country folk, who thought they were comets. He marked the passage of the sun in the yard of his lodging and made sundials. Although time spent like this sometimes made him lose his place in class, he was clever enough to regain it as soon as he set his mind to it.

When Isaac was fourteen years old, the Reverend Smith died and his mother returned to Woolsthorpe with the three children born from her second marriage. Newton had to leave the King's School of Grantham and return home, because as the eldest son, he was expected to manage the farm. But he soon convinced his mother that he would never make a good farmer. Sent to graze the sheep, he was often found beneath a hedge with a book, completely unaware that the sheep had wandered away. When he went into Grantham on market day to sell farm produce and buy things for the family, he would leave the job to the trusted servant who went with him and hide himself in the garret of his old lodging to read books until the servant came back. Either his Grantham schoolmaster or a maternal uncle persuaded his mother that it would be a loss for Isaac to bury his talent by making him a farmer. So it was decided that Isaac should go back to Grantham and prepare for higher education at a college.

Conflict in England

The years of Isaac Newton's childhood and early youth were stormy ones in English history. In the year Newton was born, a civil war began in England between supporters of King Charles I (known as Royalists, or Cavaliers) and those who backed the British Parliament (known as Parliamentarians, or Roundheads). Many of those who supported Parliament were members of a Protestant Christian religious group known as the Puritans. The Puritans wanted to rid the Anglican church (headed by the king) of what they considered to be sacriligious Roman Catholic practices, and to oppose Catholic influence in England from other countries such as Spain and France.

The English Civil War raged from 1642 to 1646, and again from 1648 to 1651. The capture and beheading of Charles I in 1649 resulted in England, Wales, Ireland, and Scotland being ruled by Parliament as a commonwealth. In 1653, Oliver Cromwell was named Lord Protector of the commonwealth. However, Cromwell's death in 1658 threw the young government into disarray. During Isaac Newton's last month at Grantham in 1660, church bells proclaimed the restoration of the monarchy in England, and the triumphal return of the executed king's son, Charles II, to take the throne.

Newton's childhood saw the beheading of King Charles I in 1649, as depicted in a seventeenth-century woodcut.

Newton's family are unlikely to have rejoiced when the Parliamentarians defeated the king in the civil war. They are thought by most historians to have been Royalists. Yet in later life, Newton showed many of the qualities that scholars associate with the Puritans: a strong interest in the Bible, thrift, discipline, hard work, and an avoidance of noisy and uproarious company. Puritans who exhibited these qualities must have made a deep impression on Newton's character in those formative years.

Newton at Trinity

Isaac Newton was admitted to Trinity College, Cambridge, on June 5, 1661. He was already eighteen when he entered university; many boys were enrolled at sixteen or even younger, and Newton was much more set in his ways than they were. Newton was also not as financially secure as many of his younger classmates at Trinity. When his mother had married for the second time, she had insisted that Reverend Smith should set aside a sum of money for Isaac's education. However, the fund was not large enough for Newton to pay all of his expenses at the college. To earn money he worked except as "subsizar," which involved waiting upon his tutor at the dining table and doing a few other chores.

The Cambridge to which Newton came was busily adapting itself to the return of the Stuart monarchy. The two universities of Oxford and Cambridge trained the men who were at the center of affairs in state and church. When the old order was overthrown, about half of the heads of colleges and teachers (known as "fellows" or "dons") lost their posts because they would not swear an oath to the new commonwealth. Now those put in their place feared similar treatment. Square mortarboards reappeared on the heads of teachers and students in

Plague orders, 1665
[Wellcome Library, London]

Scan here to see a short lecture on the 1665–66 Great Plague of London:

place of the round caps that the Puritans had preferred. A Royalist academic joked that Puritan fellows who hastily changed their caps had solved an ancient mathematical problem. They had "squared the circle."

Historians can trace in great detail the development of Newton's ideas from the time he came to Cambridge. He seems to have kept almost every scrap of paper on which he ever wrote. This helps modern scholars to clearly understand the way Newton's mind developed.

The university required him to learn his science from the works of the famous Greek thinker, Aristotle, who had lived in the fourth century BCE. Isaac's notebooks discuss the ideas of Aristotle. But they also discuss the ideas of more recent thinkers, like Galileo Galilei of Italy and René Descartes of France. These thinkers had challenged Aristotle and suggested that nature must be studied and explained in a different way. Newton studied the ancient ideas because he would be examined on them. He was not a slavish follower of the more recent thinkers and made some shrewd criticisms. Still, he took it for granted that scientific study must now follow a different path.

TEXT-DEPENDENT QUESTIONS

1. Where did Isaac Newton attend school when he was about twelve years old?
2. What happened to King Charles I in 1649?
3. What college did Newton attend in Cambridge beginning in 1661?

RESEARCH PROJECT

The English Civil War was a major event during the early life of Isaac Newton. Using your school library or the internet, find out more about the causes of this seventeenth-century conflict. Write a two-page report and share it with your class.

The fountain, great gate, and chapel at Trinity College, one of the constituent colleges of the University of Cambridge. Trinity was founded in 1546, and Isaac Newton enrolled there in 1661.

WORDS TO UNDERSTAND

concave—a surface that curves inward, like the inside of a circle or sphere.

cosmology—a system of the universe and of the general laws that govern it.

ether—Aristotle believed this was a fifth element, which was superior to the four elements (fire, earth, air, and water) that he thought made up everything below the sphere of the moon. All stars, planets, and other heavenly bodies were made up of Ether.

CHAPTER 2
The Teachings of Aristotle

The science that Newton was taught at Cambridge University was based on the teachings of Aristotle. Some changes had been made in the thirteenth century and in the sixteenth century to make Aristotle's teachings agree with the religious beliefs of the Roman Catholic Church. Otherwise Aristotle's ideas—and thus the scientific knowledge of Europe, western Asia, and northern Africa—had remained much the same for nearly 2,000 years.

New Science Versus Old

How was it possible that one person's ideas could stop scientific advance for two millennia? Why had the Christian world accepted Aristotle since the thirteenth century as "the master of those that know," as the poet Dante Alighieri had called him? Educated Jews and Muslims in Europe, Africa, and Asia also accepted Aristotle's ideas during the Middle Ages—despite the fact that Aristotle's ideas actually clashed with the basic teachings of all three religions. Aristotle did not believe that God had created the universe out of nothing. His God did not watch over or intervene in the universe. Nor had he given men souls that survived the deaths of their bodies.

By the late seventeenth century, some people were questioning Aristotle's ideas about the world and how it worked. Joseph Glanvill, who lived at the same time as Newton, said that Aristotle's science had no support "either from sense or reason," and that it helped neither "knowledge or life." Francis Bacon, an English writer and philosopher, who had strongly opposed Aristotle's science in the early seventeenth century, tried to explain how Aristotle had come to rule men's minds. He said that when the barbarian peoples had destroyed the Roman Empire, human learning had suffered a shipwreck. All knowledge that was solid and worthwhile had sunk beneath the waves of time. Only that which was lightest and most worthless, like the systems of Aristotle and his master Plato, had floated to the surface like wooden planks.

Bacon's suggestion seems to ring true when we remember how similar the "New Science" of Galileo and Descartes was to the ideas of some ancient thinkers who had lived even before Aristotle. The "New Science" had three key features. It accepted the **cosmology**, or arrangement of the universe, put forward in the mid-sixteenth century by Nicolas Copernicus, in which the planets and the Earth moved around the sun. It believed that the greatest secrets of nature could be found by revealing the mathematics that lay at their root. And it supposed that all matter was made up of small invisible particles, and that the ways in which one piece of matter was different from another could be explained by the way in

For a short video on Aristotle's model of the universe, scan here:

The ancient Greek philosopher Aristotle (384–322 BCE) developed theories about how the universe worked that would be accepted by scientists and scholars for thousands of years.

which those particles were arranged and moved—a theory known as atomism.

All these ideas could be found in the teachings of various Greek scholars who had lived before Aristotle. During the fourth century bce, Aristarchus of Samos had argued that the Earth and the planets moved around the sun, contradicting a common belief of his time that the sun and planets moved around the Earth. In the sixth century bce, Pythagoras had been so amazed at how numbers governed music that he and his followers made a religion out of mathematics. In the fifth and fourth centuries bce, atomism had been boldly proposed by Democritus to explain the birth of the universe and, indeed, everything that happened in nature.

Why had men turned their backs for centuries on what might seem very promising beginnings, and accepted instead the very different ideas of Aristotle?

The Importance of Aristotle

The real answer is not the one given by Bacon and others in the seventeenth century. It is that Aristotle's ideas were far closer to humans' commonsense picture of the world than any rival bodies of ideas. But Aristotle did not just dismiss these other ideas. Indeed, people know about some of them only because Aristotle discussed them in great detail. But in each case he gave reasons for believing that they were false, and his reasons seemed very strong for a long time.

Aristotle was, above all, a naturalist and biologist. He has a good claim to be called the founder of biology as a science. His study of living things made him believe that what was most striking and important about nature was the way in which everything seemed to aim at a particular target, and marched toward a goal. Every natural thing had a mature form and, when it was left free, moved toward it. The acorn became an oak, a baby became an adult man or woman. In studying living things, the most sensible question to ask about their parts was: What is it for? What function does it serve? Purpose and order marked nature in every way.

That was quite contrary to the fantastic universe that the atomists had suggested, where chance ruled everything. Could atoms moving about in an unlimited empty space and becoming entangled and separated by chance alone really have led to the marvelous purpose and order displayed by nature?

Nor did Aristotle accept mathematics as a most important tool for studying nature. It is useful to know how long and broad, thick or thin a thing is. But such information is by no means the most useful to understand what a thing is really like. Does a modern reader really know more about the snub-nose which the great Greek thinker Socrates had if it is discussed in terms of **concave** curves? Aristotle focused his attention mainly on living and growing things. Mathematics seemed to be of little help in studying them. He never realized just how much mathematics could do for science. He insisted that people ought to study the world in all its living richness, rather than the pale ghosts of mathematics.

Aristotle rejected the strange idea of Aristarchus that it was the Earth that really moved around the sun. Strong objections had already been quite reasonably made against this theory, based on human experiences. The sun rises every day on the eastern horizon and sets in the west. And if there is one thing everyone can be quite sure of, it is that the ground is still and unmoving beneath our feet.

THE MUSIC OF THE SPHERES

Aristotle's own teacher, Plato, was one of the greatest ancient thinkers. Plato developed the idea that the heavens were perfect, so he believed the stars and planets had to move in "perfect curves on perfect solids"—circles around spheres, in other words. He believed that the spheres made music as they turned, an idea that persisted for many centuries. Aristotle incorporated these ideas into his own philosophy.

Belief in celestial spheres, with the Earth at the center, persisted for a long time. Around 100 CE a book was published that summarized astronomical thinking up until then. This was the *Almagest*, written by the astronomer Ptolemy. Ptolemy's universe looked like this: the Earth was at the center, and around it, in increasing order of distance, were the Moon, Mercury, Venus, the Sun, Mars, Jupiter, and Saturn. The planets were attached to little spheres, and moved in circles called "epicycles." The little spheres were attached to larger spheres surrounding the Earth. The stars were fixed to an eighth sphere surrounding the others. As strange as this sounds, Ptolemy's system worked! It could be used to predict accurately where the planets would be in the sky and, more importantly, it gave reasons why. It would be another 1,400 years before more accurate observations made it necessary to find a better explanation.

Francis Bacon (1561–1626) was an English writer and philosopher and an opponent of Aristotle's theories of the universe. He was, like Newton, educated at Trinity College, Cambridge, England.

There were also strong physical arguments against the rapid motion of the Earth. All things not firmly attached to the Earth would be thrown off into space, like water drops on the rim of a spinning wheel. Birds and clouds would move quickly westward as the Earth left them behind. A ball dropped from a high tower would not fall vertically downward because the Earth would have moved while it was falling.

To these commonsense arguments Aristotle added others that were to carry great weight for a long time. Matter is observed on the Earth as a solid, a liquid, a gas, or as radiant. Early Greek thinkers suggested that everything on Earth was made of a mixture of four elements: earth, water, air, and fire. All four elements are present in any particular thing, but there is more of one than the others. Any one element can always be changed into another. Thus, the water we know is made of all four elements, but with an excess of the pure element water. When it is frozen, it becomes solid and is changed into earth. When heated, it turns into steam, which was taken to be air.

Aristotle made these earlier ideas more systematic. He noted that each element tended to move in a particular direction. A stone always fell down when released by the hand. Steam and fire always strove upward. The purpose and order which had so impressed Aristotle when studying living and growing things seemed to him to be present in the motions of "dead" things too. As we have already seen, he believed that the true nature of a living thing was clear if we studied the mature form toward which it moved. The "elementary" nature of a thing, similarly, was shown by the direction in which it moved when not interfered with. Each thing moved toward its natural place in the universe. If the motion of the sun did not always mix up the elements, they would in time have settled down in their proper place. There would then be an earthy nucleus, surrounded by layers of water, air, and fire in that order.

Earth at the Center

It should now be clear that for Aristotle, the Earth had to be at the center of the universe. That was the place of the heaviest and lowliest element. Newton was to ask why an apple fell down, rather than upward or sideways. Aristotle would have answered that the apple's nature was earthy, and the center of the universe was the natural place of earthy things.

The Earth could not possibly move, according to Aristotle's ideas. Things moved because they were out of their place and wanted to get back to it. The Earth was already in its proper place. "Natural" motions cease when things are in their places.

Aristotle saw two sorts of motions on the Earth. Either they are natural motions, and need no force. Or they are forced or "violent" motions, as when we throw a stone in the air, or blow down on a flame, or when a cart is pulled by a horse, or a boat rowed by oarsmen. In the second case, a push or a pull has to be supplied by a living thing, which touches the thing being pushed or pulled. Both sorts of motion have a beginning and an end. Either a thing reaches its place, or that which pushes or pulls it stops doing so after a time.

But look up at the heavens. The sun and the seven planets revolve around the Earth in unchanging circular paths. According to Aristotle, they are made up not of the four elements, as is everything below the orbit of the moon, but of the most perfect and superior of elements, the **ether**. It is right and fitting that they should move in circular paths, each with its own speed that is never too fast or too slow.

In this way, Aristotle split off the heavens from the Earth. In the heavens—the home of things made of the most perfect element—there could be no change. There was only uniform circular motion, and motion in a circle has neither beginning nor end. It is like a changeless change. The Earth, being made of an inferior element, could surely not take part in such a perfect movement. It was absurd to think that it could rotate around its axis to make night and day, and revolve around the sun to produce the changes of the seasons. These changes had already been explained by Greek astronomers as due to motion of the

Opposite page: This illustration from a European book published in 1551 depicts a view of Aristotle's universe that has been blended with Christian mythology. In this version, the Earth is at the center of a great spiral that incorporates the planets, the stars, the nine orders of the angels, leading eventually to God. This was the predominant view of the universe in Newton's time.

Schema præmissæ diuisionis.

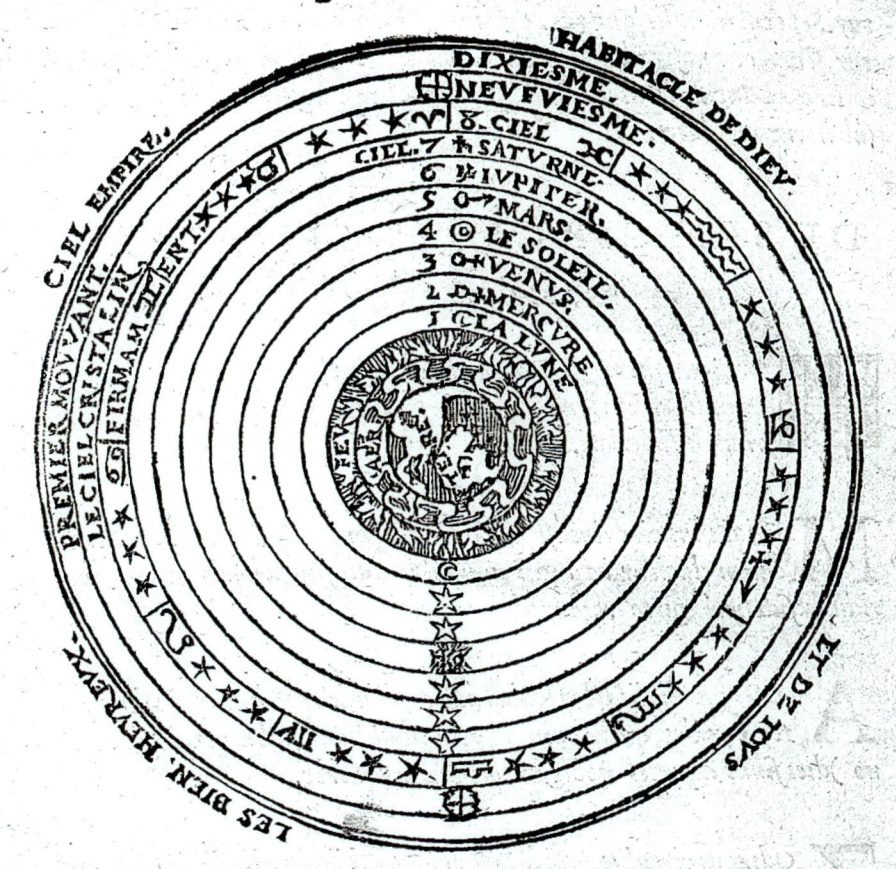

DE CIRCVLIS SPHAERAE.
CAP. III.

QVID SPHAERA.

Sphæra est solidum quoddam, vna superficie contentum, in cuius medio punctus est, à quo omnes lineæ ad circumferentiam ductæ, sunt æquales.   *Sphæra.*

Quid axis Sphæræ.

Xis Sphæræ (auctore Diodocho) vocatur

Nicolas Copernicus (1473–1543), the Polish astronomer who put forward the idea of a sun-centered universe.

whole of the heavens around the Earth once every twenty-four hours, combined with the sun's motion around the Earth in the course of a year.

Aristotle's picture of the universe may seem strange to us because we have grown up with a very different one. But this short summary of his arguments should show that he brought together, arranged, and strengthened the conclusions that had seemed reasonable to men who were no less intelligent than humans living today. The sciences about which Aristotle wrote covered a great deal. They would include what we would think of as physics, chemistry, biology, geology, astronomy and cosmology. But he wrote about much more. He wrote books on logic, or the art of reasoning, morals, politics, and poetics, which for a long time seemed to have said everything that man could possibly learn about in these fields. Aristotle had gathered together almost everything that the Greeks and other ancient civilizations like the Assyrians and Egyptians had learned. And that was done not as an encyclopedia, but in such a way that everything connected up with everything else.

The picture of the universe put forward by Nicolas Copernicus in the early sixteenth century. This arrangement had the Earth and planets moving around the sun, opposing Aristotle's view that the sun and planets moved around the Earth.

Rediscovering Aristotle

In Europe, after the fall of the Roman Empire in 476 CE, much ancient learning was lost. By the ninth century CE, few people in Christian Europe had heard of Aristotle. However, his writings were translated in Arabic and preserved by the Muslim Abbasid Empire that ruled a huge area of North Africa and the Middle East beginning around 750 CE.

As the Muslim and Christian kingdoms interacted—often through brutal wars such as the Crusades in the Middle East or the fight for control over the Iberian Peninsula, but sometimes through peaceful trade—ancient knowledge was re-introduced to Europe. By the twelfth century, the Christians had prospered and attained a cultural level that allowed them to appreciate the works of Aristotle and other ancient philosophers. Just as Jewish and Muslim scholars had, Christian thinkers—particularly the philosopher St. Thomas Aquinas (c. 1225–74)—were able to make changes in Aristotelian ideas sufficient for a time to prevent a headlong clash between them and basic Christian teachings.

By the time of Isaac Newton, a complete higher education in science could be provided by the recovered works of Aristotle, along with commentaries that suitably changed them in certain ways to conform with accepted Christian doctrine.

TEXT-DEPENDENT QUESTIONS

1. How did Aristotle's ideas clash with the basic teachings of Christianity, Judaism, and Islam?
2. What theory did Aristarchus of Samos propose in the fourth century BCE, contradicting a common belief of his time?
3. What did Aristotle believe were the five elements that made up all things?

RESEARCH PROJECT

Using the internet or your school library, find out about the accomplishments of Ptolemy, a scholar of the Roman Empire who refined Aristotle's ideas about the universe and the movement of the planets. Write a two-page report and share it with your class.

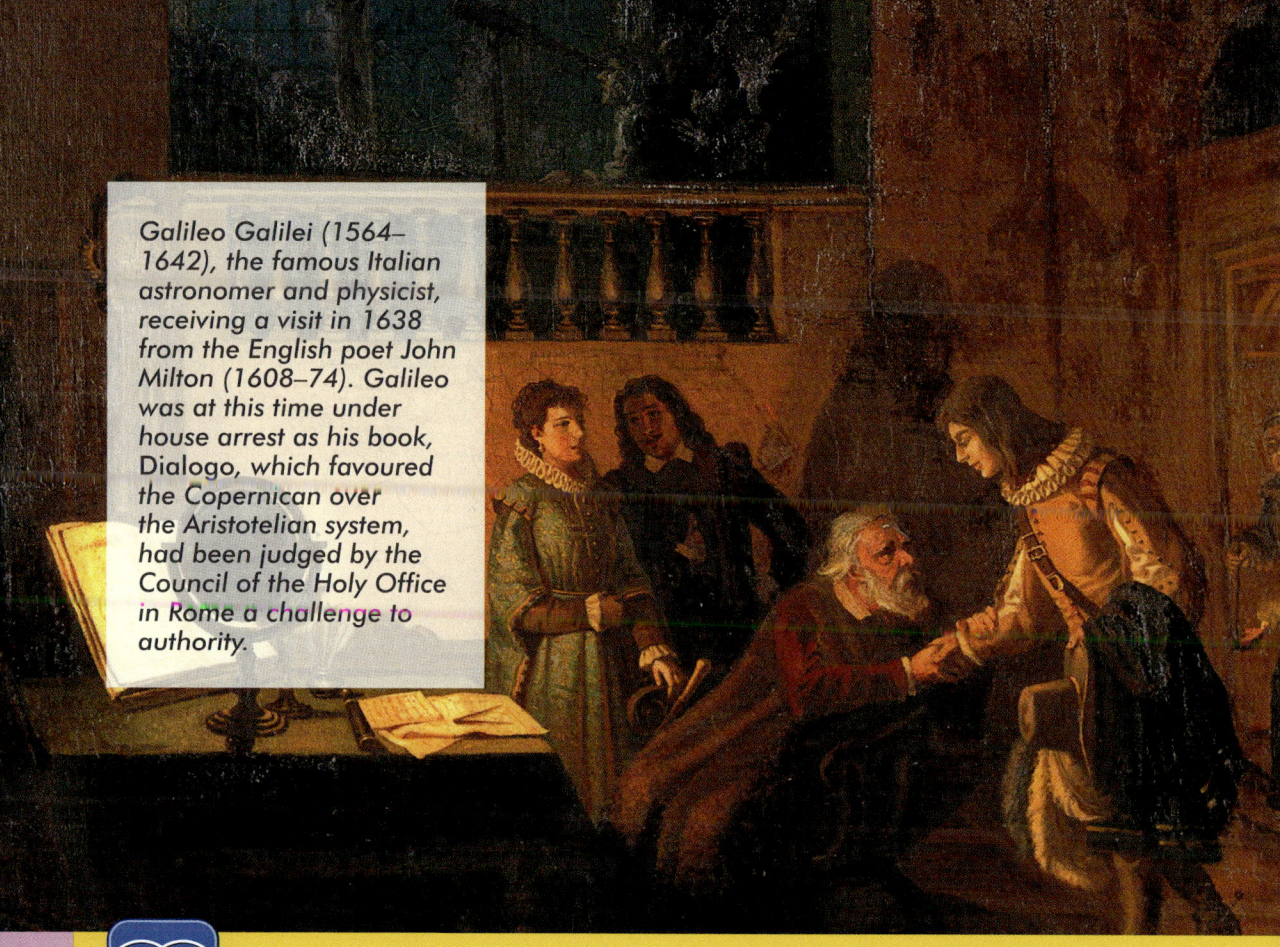

Galileo Galilei (1564–1642), the famous Italian astronomer and physicist, receiving a visit in 1638 from the English poet John Milton (1608–74). Galileo was at this time under house arrest as his book, Dialogo, which favoured the Copernican over the Aristotelian system, had been judged by the Council of the Holy Office in Rome a challenge to authority.

WORDS TO UNDERSTAND

alembic—an apparatus that consisted of two vessels connected by a tube; used by alchemists to distill chemicals by heating one of the vessels.

barometer—an instrument for measuring the weight or pressure of the atmosphere. It may be used to measure altitude, or, more commonly, to help in forecasting the weather.

laws of motion—the basic laws of the science of mechanics, like Descartes's laws of impact and pressure, or the three laws of motion given by Newton in his *Principia Mathematica*.

mechanics—the branch of applied mathematics that deals with the motions of bodies. It includes the study of the forces that cause motion, or dynamics, and the study of motion without reference to the forces causing it, or kinematics.

CHAPTER 3

The "New Science"

While he studied ancient science to satisfy Cambridge University rules, Newton was at the same time reading with excitement the works of pioneers who barely twenty years earlier had proposed new ways of explaining nature. Two men who had blazed the trail were the Italian Galileo and the Frenchman Descartes.

What made their "New Science" so different from that of Aristotle? First of all, they insisted on the most careful testing of theories by observation and experiment before they were accepted as true. A good example is a famous experiment that was being eagerly discussed when Newton was an undergraduate.

Testing the Air

Galileo had been struck by the fact that when a simple force pump was used to raise water from a well, the water never rose more than about thirty-four feet above the surface of the water. Soon after his death, his pupil Torricelli tried to explain why. Imagine that the Earth is surrounded by a sea of air. The weight of the air must press down on all things submerged in this sea, just as the sea does in our oceans. The barrel of the pump is mostly empty of air when one end is in water and the plunger is raised. The weight of the air will press down on the surface of the water and force water up the barrel. The limit on the height to which the water could be raised must then be a measure of the pressure of the air.

Torricelli did not merely put forward a theory. He thought of ways to test it. The pressure of the air supports a column of water thirty-four feet high. Torricelli reasoned that because mercury is about fourteen times heavier than water, the air should therefore support a mercury column that was 34 feet divided by 14 feet high—about 29.14 inches. Torricelli tested this theory using a glass tube that was about three feet long and sealed at one end. He filled the tube with mercury, then quickly turned it upside down in a bowl filled with mercury to create a vacuum. The mercury dropped out of the tube and into the bowl, but stopped falling when the column stood just under thirty inches high. Torricelli had tested his theory and invented the first **barometer**.

Blaise Pascal, already famous in his teens as a mathematical genius, heard about the experiment while he was in France. He thought of another test for the idea of a sea of air. A fish swimming upward from the ocean floor will feel less and less pressure. The weight and pressure of the water increases with depth. So with the sea of air. The barometer should drop as we go up a mountain, since the air pressure steadily decreases. Pascal's brother-in-law made a careful experiment. A test barometer was left at the bottom of the mountain with an assistant. Another was carried to the top of the Puy-de-Dôme, a mountain in central France. It fell nearly three inches at the top of the mountain. The mercury column in the test barometer showed no change.

Torricelli and Pascal carefully tested out the theory of the sea of air. They chose to work with exact quantities to make the experimental tests as accurate as possible. That method was a vital part of the new scientific approach. We shall see later that Newton made the most careful and exact experiments to check his theories.

But it would be wrong to conclude that only the modern thinkers believed in testing their ideas while Aristotle and other ancient philosophers had been "armchair theorists." True, Aristotle did not set up exact experimental tests. But he believed in the detailed and painstaking study of nature—that is, primarily living things—the way a field naturalist does today. So careful and original were his observations, for example on certain sea creatures, that they were not improved on till the last century.

Experiments, after all, help to answer the questions we put to nature. The sorts of

Blaise Pascal (1623–62), the French mathematician, physicist, and religious thinker who, in the late 1640s and with the help of his brother-in-law, proved experimentally the weight of air. Descartes claimed to have suggested the experiment to Pascal some years before.

René Descartes (1596–1650), the French mathematician, physicist and philosopher. His physical theories were firmly based on his philosophy, an approach to physics that Newton claimed to be quite contrary to his own, which was based on the development of theories from experiments and experimental results alone.

questions we think worth asking, the answers we find satisfying, and the tests by which we make sure that our answers are correct depend on certain ideas we begin by taking for granted. In the end, they depend on what we believe nature is like. If it is the tendency of things to aim at a goal, of living things to progress toward their mature "forms" that we take to be their most important feature, then (like Aristotle) we shall search, above all, for the "final cause" or purpose embodied in a thing. Once we have found it, our search is at an end. The test will be whether it agrees with observation, seems reasonable and satisfying to the mind, and whether we have arrived at it without making logical blunders.

A New Way of Thinking

The "New Science" made quite different assumptions. Descartes said nature was an automaton. It had to be studied not in terms of the living and growing organism, but as if it were a machine. Nature was matter in motion. That matter had certain mathematical features: size, shape, arrangement, and motion. Matter can affect other matter only by colliding with it. A scientific explanation should aim at giving us a mathematical account of nature in terms of matter in motion.

For Descartes, plants, animals, and human bodies were really marvelously constructed machines. The Earth and the planets that whirled unceasingly around the sun were parts of a heavenly clockwork. When we study machines, it makes no sense to ask what purpose they are trying to fulfill. Machines can have none except those which their makers have built into them. One piece of matter cannot have greater dignity than another, as the stars and planets had over all others for Aristotle. Nor can circular motion be superior to motion in a straight line.

Descartes tried to imagine how the world could have been born by the operation merely of the two principles of matter and motion. In the beginning God could have created matter and divided it into large chunks, which were then left to rub against each other. After that, as long as He kept the quantity of motion in the universe the same at all times, so that the machine of the universe never ran down, everything would take place purely mechanically. The rubbing of matter against other matter would in time produce three basic kinds of matter. The finest would collect and form the bodies of the sun and the stars, and swirl in immense vortices or whirlpools about them. Our sky would be made up of the second kind of rougher spherical particles. Finally, the Earth, the planets, and the comets would be made up of the roughest, irregularly shaped, and slower-moving particles.

Descartes tried to explain the movements of the Earth, planets and comets as due to the motions of the vortices. The same with gravitation on Earth. Descartes's universe was a full universe, for wherever there was space, there was matter. The vortex of particles of the second type of matter would cause a stone thrown upward to sink again to the Earth. Similar explanations were given by Descartes for such mysterious and baffling phenomena as the tides on Earth, magnetism, and the beating of the heart in the animal body.

Falling Short of the Goal

Few of Descartes's detailed and ingenious explanations are accepted today. Soon after his death, it was widely pointed out that his own work fell sadly short of the new model of doing science that he had proposed in place of the ancient one. Descartes had concluded that the most certain kind of human knowledge was mathematics. If scientific knowledge of nature was ever to become more than a matter of opinion and guesswork, it must be reduced to mathematics. That was made possible by the **mechanical** view of nature. Matter could affect other matter only by colliding with it, and all that happened in nature was due to matter in motion. Armed with a set of mathematical laws to tell us what would take place when one piece of matter collided with another—the **laws of motion** and of impact—we should be able to explain and predict everything that happened in nature.

Descartes gave plain and easily pictured analogies that may have helped to make his ideas popular. He compared the motions of the

---

Opposite page: Philippus Aureolus Theophrastus Bombastus ab Hohenheim (1493–1541), known more commonly as Paracelsus, was one of the founders of medical chemistry. This is the title page of an English translation of one of his works, Of the Supreme Mysteries of Nature.

PARACELSUS

Of the
Supreme MYSTERIES
OF
NATURE.

OF { The Spirits of the Planets.
{ Occult Philosophy.

The Magical, Sympathetical, and Antipathetical CURE of Wounds and Diseases.

The Mysteries of the twelve SIGNS of the ZODIACK.

Englished by R. Turner,
Φιλομαθής.

London, Printed by J. C. for N. Brook and J. Harison; and are to be sold at their shops at the Angel in Cornhil, and the holy Lamb neer the East-end of Pauls. 1656.

planets to that of bits of cork caught up in a whirlpool, the reflection of light to tennis balls bouncing on a hard surface, and the action of the heart to the generation of heat in hay mows. He did not work out his ideas mathematically as his own ideal of science demanded. Descartes had recognized that even if God had used only the two principles of matter and motion in running the universe, there were countless ways in which they could have been used to cause any particular phenomenon that science studied. Only experimental tests could tell us what mechanism lay behind any particular effect. But few of his own bold explanations had been put to searching experimental tests.

Despite these glaring faults that others were quick to notice, Descartes seemed to be a great liberator of the human mind to those who fell under the spell of his work. They included many very gifted young people. Why did Descartes make such a great impression upon their minds?

The "mechanical-mathematical" view of nature, which Descartes had spelt out so clearly and in so much detail, did not spring suddenly and fully formed to replace Aristotle. The subtle mixture of Aristotle and Christian doctrines by medieval churchmen had already begun to fall apart in the fourteenth and fifteenth centuries. During the Renaissance, men eagerly studied the writings of ancient

For a short video about alchemy, scan here:

Greece and Rome for models of thought and conduct. They showed contempt for the technical systems devised by churchmen with their eyes fixed wholly on the life to come. By the sixteenth century, the Aristotle whose ideas lay behind these systems was being openly attacked. His was not going to be the last word on human knowledge.

Finding an Alternative

It was one thing to attack Aristotle's system as outdated, but quite another to replace it with a new one with the same range and unity that would also be suitable as a new basis for higher education. There were endless arguments about the alternatives.

Two products of the turmoil in the world of ideas are of special interest. John Donne, the English poet and Anglican clergyman, imagined in 1611 some of the men who had overthrown long-established opinions presenting their claims before the Devil in Hell. The two men of science he chose were the Polish astronomer Copernicus and the Swiss doctor and alchemist Paracelsus. Copernicus, Donne wrote, claimed to have overturned "the whole frame of the world, and thereby ... [to be] almost a new Creator." Paracelsus had brought the whole of existing medicine into contempt, and had tried "not only to make a man ... but also to preserve him immortal."

Copernicus was the most outstanding astronomer of his time. In his masterpiece, whose first printed copy he is said to have received on his deathbed in 1543, he tried to simplify astronomy with the radical idea of having the Earth and the planets circling the sun. This, he said, explained all changes seen in the heavens; he reworked the calculations by which astronomers predicted the motions of sun, moon, and planets. But he had no real answer for the physical objections to a moving Earth that had been put forward in ancient times. Copernicus could be accepted only when a new physics, compatible with a rotating and revolving Earth, had been created to take the place of that of Aristotle.

Quite different was the reform attempted by Paracelsus. For centuries, alchemists had tried to turn base metals into gold. They claimed that Aristotle's ideas supported this endeavor. If every thing developed toward its perfect form, then the metals "growing" in the Earth must be ripening toward the form of gold. The alchemist wished to speed up that process by using a ferment, like the yeast used in bread-making and brewing. That ferment, called the "philosopher's stone," later came to be regarded as a "universal elixir." If it could be discovered, this elixir would rid men of all diseases, just as it rid metals of their imperfections. Paracelsus's achievement was to turn alchemy away from the search for transmutation to chemical remedies for diseases. He tried to read all nature in terms of the reactions that boiled and bubbled in the flasks and **alembics** of the alchemist's laboratory.

Paracelsus insisted that knowledge of nature must come from direct experience, not from the writing of Aristotle. That knowledge was to be used for human welfare. These ideas have a modern ring. Aristotle and the schoolmen had placed too much confidence in the power of human reason alone to penetrate the mysteries of nature. They had ignored the careful checks and experiments on which the "New Science" insisted. Knowledge to them was for gratifying man's wonder and curiosity, rather than to furnish him with useful inventions and discoveries. But the loss of confidence in Aristotle during the Renaissance often went with a revived belief in the "magic" of the ancient world. The stars were thought to govern our world; man had the power to tap their power and work wonders by a knowledge deeper than that brought about by using mere reason. The ideas of Paracelsus were tied to these magical beliefs.

There were many voices calling on men to follow different paths, if the old beaten road of Aristotle was to be abandoned. When the old order in church and state was overthrown in England between 1640 and 1660, some of those who wished to reform education and society suggested replacing Aristotelian science at the English universities with a Paracelsian one.

That helps to explain the wide appeal of Descartes. At one stroke he seemed to have cut through the tangled forest of Aristotelian-scholastic ideas, while avoiding the mystical twilight by which many sought a new way to true knowledge of nature. His mechanical account of all that Aristotle had explained in nature gave others confidence in attempting a different account, even if his own explanations had to be improved or thrown out.

An alchemist works in his laboratory. The shelves and tables are covered with books, flasks, and alembics. Newton had a strong interest in alchemy.

Robert Boyle (1627–91) was one of the outstanding fellows of the Royal Society, making important contributions in physics, chemistry, and medicine. Boyle is best known for his work on the properties of air. He differed from Newton in his views on light and color, and also on alchemy.

In England the new program captured the enthusiasm of a group of brilliant young men. They included Robert Boyle, a younger son of the Earl of Cork; his assistant, Robert Hooke, who was later to quarrel bitterly with Newton; and Christopher Wren, who advised on the rebuilding of London after the Great Fire of 1666 and designed St. Paul's Cathedral. At the Restoration, these men founded the Royal Society for the Promotion of Natural Knowledge, which adopted the way of explaining nature mechanically. "New Science" seemed to have become respectable and had caught the interest and patronage of King Charles II and fashionable society.

TEXT-DEPENDENT QUESTIONS

1. Which two influential scientists blazed the trail for the "New Science"?
2. How did Descartes try to explain the movements of planets and stars?
3. What is the philosopher's stone?

RESEARCH PROJECT

Choose one of the influential scientists mentioned in this chapter, including Descartes, Galileo, Torricelli, Pascal, Copernicus, or Paracelsus. Using your school library or the internet, find out more about this person and his discoveries. Write a two-page report and share it with your class.

Although Descartes had made a valiant attempt to explain the formation of rainbows, it was left to Newton to provide a full explanation in terms of the dependence of refraction on color.

WORDS TO UNDERSTAND

aberration—the failure of an optical system to make the rays of light come to one focus. A spherical abberation is due to flaws in the lens, such as varying thickness. A chromatic aberration occurs because the different colors that make up white light are bent differently as they pass through the lens, making the resulting image fuzzy.

convex—a curve that bulges out, rather than in.

refraction—the change of direction of a ray of light as it passes from one transparent medium to another, as from air to water. If something is *refrangible*, it is capable of being refracted.

the Sine Law of Refraction—when a ray of light strikes obliquely the surface that separates two transparent media, it is bent in such a way that the sine of the angle of incidence to the sine of the angle of refraction is always constant for those two media.

spectrum—the colored band into which a beam of light is decomposed by means of a prism.

CHAPTER 4

Light and Color

Like many other gifted young men, Newton had felt the thrill of seeing the world in the new light of Descartes's work. He was eager to try his powers in the exciting adventure that science seemed to offer. At the same time, he understood Descartes's shortcomings. His ideas did not have the mathematical form that Newton's own ideal demanded. Nor had they been put to rigorous experimental test. In his undergraduate notes, Newton sketched perpetual motion machines that drew their power from Descartes's whirling subtle matter. But he also noted that Descartes's explanations of tides on Earth by the action of that matter did not agree with the way they actually occurred.

Soon after he graduated, Newton tackled the basic problem that had to be solved before the new physics of matter and motion could be more than a dream. The mechanical system had explained all changes in nature as changes in the position and motion of material bodies. Some mathematical way had to be found of explaining that process of change. The crucial problem was to measure how quickly one quantity in a situation changes in relation to another quantity. Velocity, for example, is the rate of change of distance with respect to time. Acceleration is the rate of change of that rate of change, or how quickly velocity increases. Newton's mathematical genius took wings. He laid the basis of what we now call differential and integral calculus, and so gave physics its most powerful mathematical tool. By differentiation it was possible to measure how quickly one changing

Isaac Barrow (1630–77) was a mathematics professor at Cambridge who served as a mentor for Newton.

quantity changed in relation to another at any given point in a process. Integration was the reverse process, just as subtraction is the reverse of addition. If we know the rate of change, we can find the changing quantities involved by integration.

Newton's experimental cunning and precision were to be shown in his paper on light and colors that marked his sensational entrance upon the stage of science. All these qualities were to meet in his supreme discovery, the Law of Universal Gravitation. This was to realize the dream of a physics compatible with Copernicus that had inspired men like Galileo and Descartes.

Working on the Problem

The roots of these epochal discoveries lay in the two-year period (1665–66) that included the Great Plague and the Great Fire of London. Newton seems to have owed little to his formal education or teachers. He was almost entirely self-taught. University teaching was lax. Too many of the fellows were appointed as a reward for royal services, or were waiting for better jobs as clergymen elsewhere.

Newton himself became a fellow soon after returning to a Cambridge freed

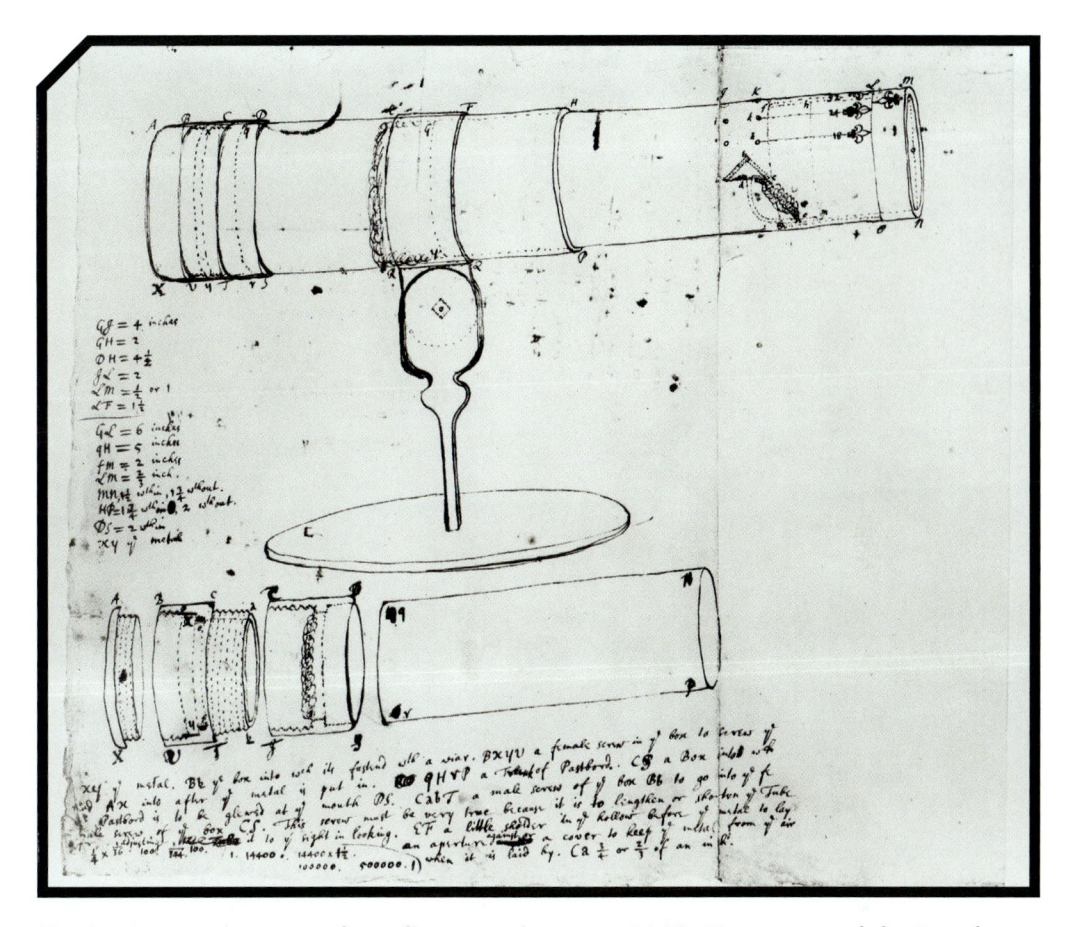

Newton's own drawing of a reflecting telescope, 1668. He presented the Royal Society with a similar one in 1671. This instrument almost totally eliminated chromatic aberration, as the Law of Reflection is the same for all colors. A very small amount of splitting of colors occurred at the eyepiece.

of the Plague. His achievements won the admiration of a senior member of his college, Isaac Barrow, the Lucasian Professor in Mathematics. Barrow asked Newton's help in revising his own optical lectures for printing, and praised him in letters to his London friends. Newton was chosen soon afterward to succeed him in the Lucasian Chair in Mathematics. A reflecting telescope made by Newton reached the Royal Society. Newton sent them the telescope as a gift. It created

This statue of Newton was erected at Trinity College in Cambridge in 1775.

some excitement. Charles II is said to have looked through it. Newton was soon elected a fellow of the Society.

Newton was pleased by the Society's appreciation. In a letter to the secretary, Henry Oldenburg, he revealed that he had a far richer gift to offer than a telescope: a whole new theory of light and colors that had led him to make the instrument. Newton knew the importance of his discovery. He called it "the oddest, if not the most considerable detection, which hath hitherto been made in the operations of Nature."

The short paper Newton sent some weeks later is one of the most famous documents in the history of science. The opening passage conveys its flavor: "To perform my late promise to you, I shall without further ceremony acquaint you, that in the beginning of the Year 1666 (at which time I applyed myself to the grinding of Optick glasses of other figures than Spherical), I procured me a Triangular glass-prism, to try therewith the celebrated Phaenomena of Colours. And in order thereto having darkened my chamber, and made a small hole in my window-shuts, to let in a convenient quantity of the sun's light, I placed my Prism at its entrance, that it might be **refracted** to the opposite wall. It was at first a very pleasing divertisement, to view the vivid and intense colours produced thereby; but after a while applying myself to consider them more circumspectly, I became very surprised ..."

The threads lead from this account, once more, back to Descartes. In his first published work, Descartes had taken the problems of light as a challenge to and test of his new method. Even in ancient times, optics had been found to be a science well suited to mathematical treatment. Moreover, ancient and medieval writers had found it useful when working out problems to think of light rays as if they were balls hitting a surface. These features fitted perfectly into Descartes's studies. He derived the **Sine Law of Refraction** by imagining light rays as tennis balls striking a surface. He explained the formation of the rainbow.

Descartes did not believe that light was really made up of tiny solid particles. He thought of it as the pressure through the ether of the luminous matter that made up the bodies of the sun and the stars. The ordinary laws of mechanics applied to that pressure. How were colors to be explained? The "New Science" assumed that sensations like color, taste, smell, and touch were due to the more basic mathematical features of matter. Descartes said that we see colors through the action on our optic nerve of "ethereal globules" that are set spinning like tops when they obliquely strike an object. Different speeds of rotation give rise to different colors.

Making a Better Telescope

One important reason for the new interest in optics was the improvement of telescopes. Galileo had made one in about 1609 after hearing reports of its invention. It consisted of an object lens, to form the image of a distant object, and an eyepiece to magnify the image. Galileo pointed his instrument at the heavens and made several surprising discoveries, which he used to support Copernicus. Descartes had looked at the difficulties in improving the telescope. The chief one arose from what would now be called **spherical aberration**. The lens gave a fuzzy image because light rays from the top and bottom ends of the lens did not come to a sharp focus with the other rays. Descartes suggested that the solution was to grind lenses of non-spherical shapes. That was why Newton in 1666 was trying what proved the near impossible task of grinding lenses "of other figures than spherical."

HOW A PRISM WORKS

A prism is a transparent type of optical lens, often in a triangle shape, with flat, polished surfaces. In Newton's time, prisms were made of glass. The effects of a prism occur because light changes speed as it moves from one medium (such as air) to another (into the glass of the prism). The speed change, as well as the angles in the prism, cause the light to be bent, or refracted. Light of different colors is bent differently, so it leaves the prism at different angles. This creates an effect similar to a rainbow.

When Newton tried out the prism experiment, what first surprised him was the shape of the **spectrum** on the wall. It was oblong, and about five times as long as it was broad. He had expected to see the round image of the sun. He made careful experiments to find out why.

He passed the beam through various parts of the prism to see if the thickness of the glass affected the result. The shape stayed the same. To make sure the beam had not been scattered by a flaw in the glass, he placed another prism upside down behind the first one. By doing this any changes in the light beam due to its triangular shape would be cancelled out. However, if the image had been altered because of a flaw in the glass, the changes would be even greater. Newton would have seen a longer oblong and perhaps a greater splitting up of colors. In fact, the image became round again, as if the beam had not passed through a prism at all.

Could the shape be due to rays from different parts of the disc of the sun meeting the prism from different angles? Precise calculations showed that this could not possibly have led to such a large angle between the emerging rays. Could it be that the rays moved not in a straight but in a curved line when they emerged from the prism? Newton remembered (and there is a strong link here with Descartes's ideas) that he had "often seen a Tennis-ball, struck with an oblique racket, describe such a curved line." By letting the image fall on a board at various distances from the prism, he showed that light rays must travel in straight lines.

Having rejected these possibilities through experiments, Newton now tried what he called his "crucial experiment." He fixed a board with a small opening behind his prism. About twelve feet away, he fixed another board with a small hole, and placed a second prism behind it. By letting in a beam of light, and turning the prism over he could select a ray of a single color from the band of colors on the second board to pass through the second prism. Newton found that a ray of any one color was unchanged by the second prism. But the lower colors of the first image were bent, or refracted, more than the higher ones by the second prism.

This led Newton to a revolutionary conclusion, quite the opposite of what the ancient philosophers—as well as his fellow men of science, like Barrow—believed about colors: "The true cause of length of that Image was detected to his discovery followed a much more twisting path than his simplified version suggested. It combined hard, critical examination of existing theories with bold speculations and careful experiments.

Newton's paper created a great stir when the Royal Society read it. But it involved him in arguments that soured his spirit. He thought he had agreed to share a great discovery with the world only to find himself misunderstood. He had given up "my quiet to run after a shadow."

His critics agreed that to have shown that different colors were differently refracted was a big step forward in optical science. But they questioned his conclusion that the various colors were originally contained in the white light. Robert Hooke said light consisted of a large number of "vibrations," and each vibration produced a different color when separated out by a prism. The great Dutch follower of Descartes, Christiaan Huygens, later put forward a wave theory much better worked out than Hooke's to give an explanation along these lines.

Replying to his critics, Newton patiently pointed out the ways in which his experimental findings clashed with their different theories. But he was also led to argue as if his own conclusions had resulted purely from experiments. His critics, he said, were prejudiced because they had begun with theories and did not want to give them up. By arguing in this way, Newton was belittling the imagination involved in every great scientific discovery. It made it possible for a misleading view of science, which regards its laws and theories as no more than summaries of unprejudiced experiments and observations, to appeal to Newton's example.

Opposite page: This early eighteenth century book illustration shows lens grinders at work, as well as the various stages of the process and the tools used. Though Newton recognized the problem of spherical aberration, grinding machines of his time were far too crude to grind accurately any shape with the non-spherical surfaces that he required.

55

Newton had not overlooked the possibility of correcting chromatic aberration in lenses by combining different types of glass. But a mistake in an experiment made him think that this would not "disperse" or spread out the spectrum differently. It was almost 100 years before the mistake was spotted. Dollond managed to make lenses that combined **convex** crown glass and concave flint glasses. When used as object lenses, they almost cancelled out chromatic aberration. The refracting telescope was again to be the main instrument of astronomers.

Wearied by objections, Newton wrote to Henry Oldenburg that he had considered sending more thoughts on colors to the Royal Society "but find it yet against the grain to put pen to paper any more on that subject." He would "resolutely bid adieu to it eternally ..." The objections had, however, stung him into ordering his ideas better. He was to make many more discoveries in optics. But they were to be published only in 1704, after the death of his old adversary, Hooke.

Neil DeGrasse Tyson speaks about Newton's discoveries:

TEXT-DEPENDENT QUESTIONS

1. What gift did Isaac Newton send to the Royal Society?
2. What is spherical abberation?
3. What Dutch scientist put forth a wave theory of light?

RESEARCH PROJECT

Tape a white piece of paper to a wall, making sure it is flat and smooth, across the room from a sunny window. Hold a prism up in front of the paper, making sure to catch the light from the window. Twist and turn the prism in the light source so that light falls on the paper. Turn the prism until a corner of the triangle falls into the light beam. Light should refract through the prism and create a rainbow on the white background.

A descendent of the apple tree in the court at Trinity College, University of Cambridge, under which Newton is said to have sat when an apple fell and set him thinking about gravity.

WORDS TO UNDERSTAND

centripetal and **centrifugal force**—to make a body move in a circle, it must be pushed or pulled inward by agents like a string, a spring, or gravity. Such a force is called a centripetal or center-tending force. When a stone is whirled on a string, the string seems to pull the hand outward: that is a real centrifugal or center-fleeing force on the hand, although not on the stone, as the only force acting on it is inward. It is equal and opposite to the centripetal force of the stone.

elliptical—an elliptical orbit has the shape of an ellipse, that is, a closed curve in which the sum of the distances of any point from the two foci is a constant quantity.

inertia—the property of a body by which it tends to persist—in a state of rest or of uniform motion in a straight line.

mass—the quantity of matter in a body, as distinguished from its weight. It is the quantitative measure of inertia.

CHAPTER 5

Gravity and the Laws of Motion

The story of Newton and the apple has been told and retold. Friends heard it from his own lips in his old age. While sitting in his mother's orchard one day during the Plague year, his attention was caught by an apple falling to the ground. This set him thinking. However, twenty years were to pass before his ideas about gravity and motion were published in his *Principia Mathematica*.

Why the delay? A number of clever explanations have been given for why he kept his discovery from the world for so long. Recent historical work has changed our ideas about this. It now seems likely that the crucial idea of universal gravitation came to Newton only much later—not until after he had written the first section of his masterpiece.

Newton had already studied the problem of the motion of Earth and planets around the sun when he was an undergraduate. Aristotle had imagined a nest of hollow spheres carrying sun, moon, and planets around the Earth in their daily and yearly motions. Copernicus had not given up the spheres, but his work made others more and more reluctant to believe in them. If there were no spheres, what kept the Earth and the planets circling around the sun?

Discoveries of Kepler and Galileo

Early in the seventeenth century, the German astronomer Johannes Kepler suggested that a moving force, radiating from the sun like spokes in a wheel, carried the planets around as the sun itself spun. But he altered this model after a discovery of immense importance. Kepler was inspired by Pythagoras's belief that mathematics would lay bare the hidden nature of things. He tried to show that the observed positions of the planets were on uniform circular orbits, and he tried to do this more precisely than anyone else had done before him. After long years of hard work and failure, he came up with a solution. The ancient idea of uniform circular motion had to be abandoned. The planets moved in **elliptical orbits** (flattened circles) with the sun at one focus. In such an orbit, the speeds of the planets and their distance from the sun would change all the time. To explain this, Kepler thought of magnetic poles in the planets that were attracted or repelled by a magnetic north pole in the sun itself.

Few people took Kepler's elliptical orbits, or his "celestial mechanism," seriously for a long time. A new science of motion had to be created before his ellipses, and two other discoveries, could serve as the foundation of a new world-picture. The first great step toward it was made by another follower of Copernicus, Galileo Galilei.

Galileo is often said to have disproved Aristotle by dropping balls of different weight from the Leaning Tower at Pisa. If Aristotle's theories were right, the heavier ball should have struck the ground first. Galileo showed that both balls reached the ground at the same time. The story may or may not be true. It is certainly not a good illustration of Galileo's importance to science. His great achievement was to single out the vital features of physical events in a real-life situation—like a falling stone, or a swinging pendulum—and to "think away" the rest. By doing this he clarified ideas like speed, acceleration, and resistance.

Aristotle had stuck close to common experience. He thought that, except for "natural" motions, all movement needed a mover. If the mover stopped pushing, the movement would stop. Galileo "thought away" friction and imagined a perfectly smooth ball being placed upon an ideally smooth slope. The ball would roll faster and faster down the slope. On an upward slope, force would be needed to push it along or even to hold it still. Therefore, on an endless level surface, there is no reason why a ball once set moving should ever stop.

The principle of **inertia** to which Galileo pointed was a big break with ancient

Johannes Kepler (1571–1630), the German astronomer and physicist famous for his laws of planetary motion, that provided the basis for much of Newton's work. Kepler thought that the forces that took the planets in fixed orbits around the sun were something akin to magnetism in nature.

thought. Motion as such does not need a continuous force to keep it going. Only a change of motion needs force. Galileo used this principle to answer ancient objections to a moving Earth. A stone would not cease to share the motion of the Earth the moment it lost contact with it. When dropped from a high tower, it would drop to the foot of the tower because it would really have two motions: one downward, the other a circular one shared with the moving Earth. The power of old ideas, even on those trying to break with them, is shown by Galileo's continuing to think of these motions as "natural." Circular motion remained perfect motion for him; only now earthy matter could share this perfection too.

A New Way of Thinking

It was Descartes who sharply rejected such ideas. Inertial motion was uniform motion in a straight line. Circular motion was not natural, but needed a mechanical cause. For the Earth and the planets, said Descartes, that cause was the "Whirlpool of subtle matter" that carried them around the sun. That same power explained why a stone, when let go, dropped to the ground. The subtle matter in the Earth's vortex moved away much faster and the stone, like a piece of wood in a watery whirlpool, was driven to the center.

If it was the fall of an apple that set Newton thinking in 1666 about the power needed to hold the moon around the Earth and the planets around the sun, he probably thought of it as due to these Cartesian vortices. When we whirl a stone in a sling, the tension in the string may seem to us a sign of the stone's tendency to fly away. It came to be called a **centrifugal**, or center-fleeing, tendency. Newton worked out a way of calculating it, and estimated what it was for the Earth, moon, and planets. It then occurred to him to combine it with something that Kepler had discovered. Kepler had found that the time (T) taken by a planet to orbit the sun varied and depended on its average distance (D) from the sun in such a way that the ratio T_2/D_3 was the same for all planets. That meant, Newton discovered, that the "centrifugal" tendency of the planets must vary inversely as the square of their distance from the sun.

It has usually been assumed that Newton must have thought of the centrifugal tendency as balanced by a gravitational force that acts from the sun upon the

Earth and the planets. As that force is universal, it should be possible to test the effect of the Earth's gravitational force upon the moon. The moon's inertial motion would carry it with uniform speed in a straight line. It orbits the Earth because it is continuously pulled away from that path by the Earth's gravitation. Newton knew that at the surface of the Earth, that gravitational pull causes objects, such as apples, to fall sixteen feet in the first second after starting from rest. If the pull decreases according to the inverse-square law, then at the distance of the moon, its force would be 1/3600 of that on the Earth. An object on the moon must then take one minute to fall the distance it fell in one second on the Earth. So according to gravity, the moon should be pulled away from its straight inertial path by sixteen feet every minute.

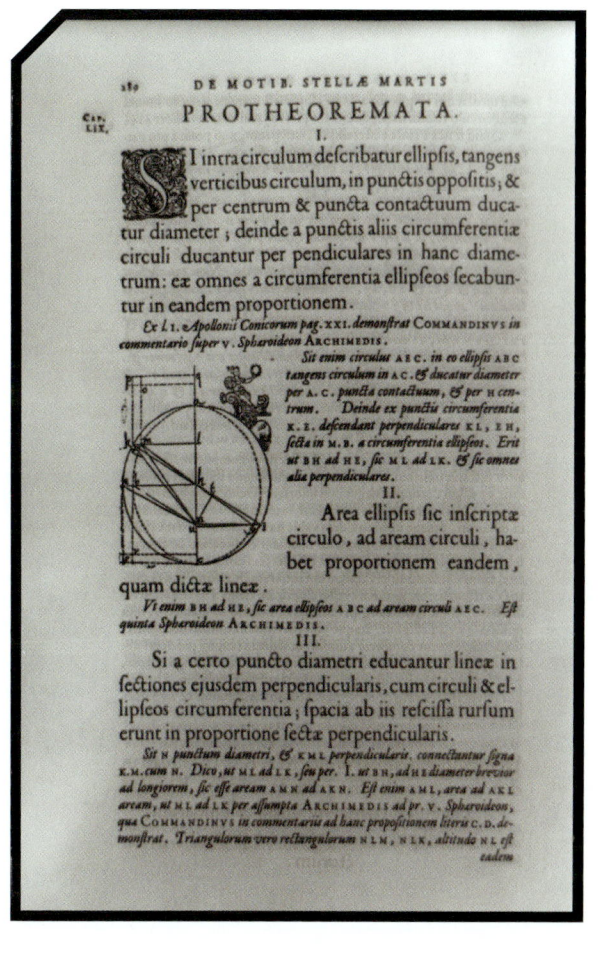

Diagrams from Kepler's Astronomia Nova *("New Astronomy," 1609) in which, after an immense amount of work, he set out his discovery of the Law of Elliptical Orbits for planets. The diagram describes the elliptical orbit of Mars.*

Newton tested the result by a simple calculation. He worked out the moon's acceleration from its period of revolution and the supposed size of its orbit around the Earth. He then compared the acceleration worked out in this way, with that given by the inverse-square relation. The answer agreed "pretty nearly," but not

A meeting of the Royal Society in Crane Court, Fleet Street, presided over by Newton.

exactly, because he used too small a figure for the size of the Earth. A moon-test by Newton, probably done in 1666, has been found among his writings, but there is no suggestion there that he had yet begun to think of the inward force as a gravitational attraction between sun and planets, or Earth and moon.

Returning to the Problem

Newton put aside work on these problems until brought back to them in 1679 by Robert Hooke, who had now become secretary of the Royal Society. Hooke asked him to suggest problems to revive public interest in science. Hooke wrote to Newton suggesting that if a body orbited the Earth so that it was attracted by the Earth with a force varying inversely as the square of the distance, its path would be an ellipse with the Earth at one focus. Hooke offered no mathematical proof. Newton later claimed that he had worked out a proof but had tossed the paper aside, "being upon other studies."

In 1684 Edmond Halley visited Newton in Cambridge. Halley had found that Hooke and Sir Christopher Wren, like himself, had guessed that Kepler's sun-planet relation meant that there is an inverse-square attraction between sun and planets. None of them could offer a mathematical proof. Hooke claimed one, but did not take up Wren's wager of a book worth forty shillings.

Halley was delighted when Newton told him not only that he had made the same discovery, but that he had proved it mathematically for elliptical orbits. He could not find the proof among his papers, but promised to reconstruct it. The result was a tract that Halley saw on a second visit some months later. Newton's mathematical genius was displayed in his solution of a problem that had baffled the others. But the crucial idea of universal gravitation, which appears in the *Principia*, was still absent from this tract. To appreciate his final achievement, it is necessary to understand the problems he faced.

Robert Hooke saw that the principle of inertia meant that a force must be acting whenever a body moves in any way other than with uniform motion in a straight line. For example, circular motion needs a force to act continuously toward the center of the circle. Instead of concentrating upon supposed "centrifugal" forces arising from orbital motion, Hooke pointed to the force that made a body travel in such a path. For the Earth and the planets, Hooke suggested that this force was an attraction toward the center of the sun.

But a deflecting force of that sort was unacceptable to "mechanical philosophers." Galileo had rejected Kepler's ideas of an attractive force from the sun. He had even denied the old idea that the attraction of the moon causes tides on Earth, and he stubbornly defended his own theory that tides were caused by the Earth's rotation. Descartes criticized Roberval for explaining the fall of heavy bodies to Earth by attraction. He could not conceive of a force acting at a distance as gravitational force was supposed to do: there must be a mechanical explanation. Such ideas seemed to Galileo and Descartes to belong to the magical tendencies that had gripped the Renaissance imagination as the hold of Aristotle slackened.

Newton himself had up to now been faithful to Descartes's system of explaining all that happened in nature by matter in motion. His acceptance of the idea of gravitational attraction plunged him into controversies to the end of his life. He could not decide whether to explain gravity as due to the direct action of God, or as due ultimately to matter in motion. What first caused him to consider such a departure?

One reason may have been the chemical and alchemical studies on which he spent so much of his time and which have continued to puzzle historians. Newton was deeply impressed by the way some chemical substances seem to have

NEWTON'S RIVAL

Robert Hooke was born in 1635. He was educated by his father, who was director of a local school, and later studied in London. When he was eighteen years old, he began studies at Oxford University. He also developed a lifelong passion for science and became friends with others who shared this passion, including architect Christopher Wren, Anglican clergyman John Wilkins, and chemist Robert Boyle, all of whom were among the founders of the Royal Society in 1662.

Hooke worked as Boyle's assistant from 1655 until about 1663. In 1664 the Royal Society appointed him to a position as curator of experiments. In this capacity he both demonstrated his own ideas, and developed experiments to test the ideas of other scientists. One area that Hooke became particularly noted for was his use of microscopes. In 1665 he made the important discovery that living things are made up of tiny individual units. He was examining a very thin slice of cork through a microscope and saw that the cork was made up of a pattern of tiny rectangular holes. He described them as "much like a honeycomb…these pores or cells, were not deep but consisted of an attraction for certain others and readily combine with them. Certain other things were difficult to explain by mechanisms of the Cartesian sort. Why does matter stick together and not just fall apart? Why does water rise in thin glass tubes? Why are light rays bent away from their paths when they enter another substance, and how can flies walk on water without wetting their feet? Attractions and repulsions between particles of matter could explain all this more simply.

Was that a backward step? Not, Newton thought, if we could discover the small number of mathematical laws presumably ruling such attractions and repulsions. Matter and motion are not enough to explain nature. In addition, there must be

a great many little boxes." Hooke's "little boxes" were actually the outermost boundaries of the once-living plant cells and were all that remained after the cell had died. The word "cell" was kept to describe the entire living cell. Hooke eventually became president of the Royal Society.

Like Newton, Hooke worked on problems involving light, gravitation, and the planets. The two men shared some of their ideas, but were also rivals who argued bitterly over which of them deserved the credit for developing them. Hooke argued with many other scientists of the time as well, and was described by his peers as arrogant.

When Hooke died in 1703, Newton succeeded him as president of the Royal Society. Newton's supporters downplayed many of Hooke's claims and accomplishments, and over the years he was overlooked in favor of Newton, Wren, Boyle, and other major scientists of the seventeenth century. It was not until the twentieth century that scholars began to more fully appreciate the importance of Hooke's scientific discoveries.

Edmond Halley (1656–1742) made a major contribution to astronomy: the study of comets. After noting the similarity of the orbits of comets that had appeared in 1456, 1531, 1607 and 1682, he concluded that they were one and the same comet and predicted to within five months its return at the end of 1758. (Bottom) Image of Halley's comet on its most recent pass by Earth, February-March 1986. The comet is scheduled to pass Earth again in 2061.

certain "active principles" planted by God in nature. Without their continuing action, nature would have come to a standstill long ago. Newton's scientific and religious thoughts came together in this view of nature that he was developing. He was deeply influenced by the thinkers known as the Cambridge Platonists. They believed that if the universe was thought of as a clockwork that God had created but then left to run itself by mechanical principles, then men would stop believing in religion. His thoughts already seem to have been moving away from purely Cartesian explanations of nature just at the time when he began once again to think about the movements of the heavens.

What Is Gravity?

If the sun pulls on the planets with a gravitational force, is this a force that acts between particular bodies (like the specific attractions in the chemical reactions Newton had studied)? Or did all matter attract all other matter? Newton decided that the force was universal.

How was the pull related to the largeness or smallness of bodies? In answering that, Newton made the first clear distinction between weight and **mass**. The weight of a body measures the gravitational pull, which will vary with distance from the center of the Earth. The mass is the "quantity of matter" in a body. A body may weigh less at the top of a high mountain, but its mass need not have changed.

Mass and weight must be exactly proportional at a fixed distance from the center of the Earth. Kepler's law connecting the distances of the planets from the sun with the time they took to orbit it meant that if all the planets were placed at the same distance from the sun, they would move in the same orbit. Newton realized that this would happen only if the pull of the sun was exactly proportional to their very different masses. It would pull, say, four times as hard on a body four times as massive as another at the same distance.

Galileo had scandalized Aristotelians by saying that, if it were not for air resistance, all bodies falling from the same height would have the same speeds. Newton now showed that to achieve this, the gravitational force would have to pull harder on a more massive body, since there was more matter to be moved.

Had the strength of the pull been the same, the lighter body would have fallen faster. It was a surprising fact that the pull was, in fact, exactly proportional to the mass of bodies. Newton further tested the proportionality by experimenting with pendulums, whose usefulness in dealing with problems of falling bodies had already been seen by Galileo. Galileo had also shown that the speed of a falling body increases regularly with time (uniform acceleration). This could now be shown to illustrate the general principle that a constant force produces, not a constant velocity as in the old physics, but a constant increase in velocity.

When calculating forces between massive bodies at great distances, like the sun and the planets, or the Earth and the moon, it was possible to treat them as "mass-points." But calculating the forces upon, say, an apple falling to the Earth, seemed to be very complicated. Parts of the Earth near at hand would pull hard, while other parts would pull with a force that became weaker at a distance. Using his new mathematical tool of fluxions, Newton proved that such massive and solid spheres attracted things as if their mass was concentrated at their centers. In this way the problems involved were enormously simplified.

Gravitation was a **centripetal** force. A more general idea of force was needed to create a workable science of dynamics—that is, a science of

To hear a humorous song that teaches about gravity, scan here:

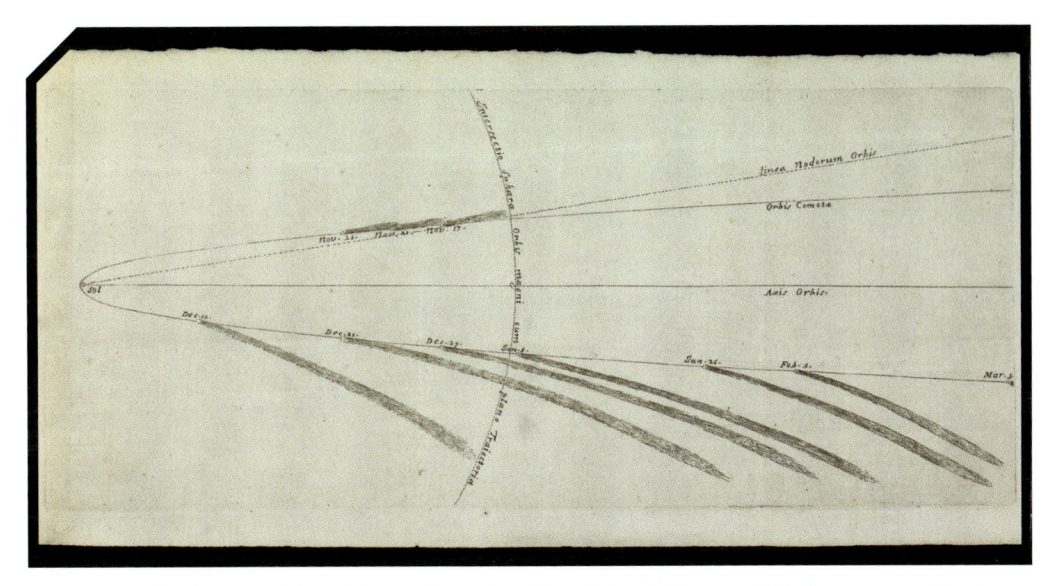

Newton's diagram of the elliptical path of the "Great Comet" that appeared in 1680–81. Newton used the comet's path to test and verify Kepler's laws of planetary motion.

motion and moving things. That was a very tough problem that had defeated earlier pioneers. There were so many different ideas of forces, measured in very different ways. Newton's true genius comes across in the simplicity of his solution. All matter possessed "inertia"—the power of resisting motion when at rest, or changes (of direction and magnitude) when in motion. Gravitation was an example of an "impressed" force that changed inertial motion. Forces, said Newton, must be proportional to, and can be measured by, the changes they cause in such inertial motion.

Three Laws of Motion

Newton set out the basic laws of his new mechanics in three laws of motion. The first stated that every body continues in its state of rest or of uniform motion in a straight line unless made to change that state by forces impressed upon it. The second law related the increase in velocity of a body to the impressed force: the acceleration gained by a body is proportional to the force and inversely proportional to its mass. The third law stated that to every action, there is an equal and opposite reaction.

Newton now applied his new ideas to a great range of problems. Besides free fall and impact, he analyzed the much harder problems of resistance, wave motion, and the motion of fluids. He tackled the "three-body" problem—that is the problem of orbital motions where more than two bodies are involved. The motions of the Earth and the planets were obviously of this sort. He was able to explain the tides, as well as the long-term motion of the axis of the Earth that produced a "precession of the equinoxes" in the heavens, and predicted a bulge at the Earth's equator.

Newton struck the death-blow to Cartesian vortices in the course of his investigations. He worked out that they would lose motion continuously and could not carry on for very long. Nor could any Cartesian "subtle matter" explain gravitation. The presence of an atmosphere even as thin as that of the Earth in interplanetary space would make Jupiter lose one-tenth of its motion in thirty days. Instead of the full universe of Descartes, Newton's was an almost empty universe, where the emptiness throughout space and within physical objects quite overshadowed the small parcels of matter scattered through its vast reaches.

These mammoth achievements were the result of just two years' work. By April 1686 the manuscript of the Mathematical Principles of Natural Philosophy was before the Royal Society. Halley decided to print it at his own expense when the Society found itself unable to pay for it. Besides his financial sacrifice, Halley

Opposite page: The title page of Newton's Principia Mathematica Philosophia Naturalis *(Mathematical Principles of Natural Philosophy), published in 1687. Edmond Halley, whose constant encouragement Newton had received while preparing the manuscript, paid for its publication out of his own pocket when the Royal Society found itself unable to pay for it.*

PHILOSOPHIÆ
NATURALIS
PRINCIPIA
MATHEMATICA.

Autore *JS.* NEWTON, *Trin. Coll. Cantab. Soc.* Matheseos Professore *Lucasiano,* & Societatis Regalis Sodali.

IMPRIMATUR.
S. PEPYS, *Reg. Soc.* PRÆSES.
Julii 5. 1686.

LONDINI,
Jussu *Societatis Regiæ* ac Typis *Josephi Streater.* Prostant Venales apud *Sam. Smith* ad insignia *Principis Walliæ* in Cœmiterio D. *Pauli,* aliosq; nonnullos Bibliopolas. Anno MDCLXXXVII.

also had to soothe Robert Hooke, who now accused Newton of stealing the inverse-square law from him. "Philosophy," Newton sadly commented, "is such an impertinently litigious Lady, that a man had as good be engaged in lawsuits, as to have to do with her." Halley had a hard time persuading Newton not to leave out the section *System of the World* which was the crown of his work.

The great work was published in May 1687 and created an immediate sensation. Even the followers of Descartes, who rejected its central idea of an attractive gravitational force, came in time to recognize its achievement. The dream of a mathematical science of nature was at last set on firm foundations, even if at its heart lay a type of action that the founders of the mechanical philosophy had wished to banish from any rational system of science.

TEXT-DEPENDENT QUESTIONS

1. What did Kepler discover about the orbital motion of the planets?
2. Who was president of the Royal Society in 1679?
3. Is gravity a centrifugal or a centripetal force?

RESEARCH PROJECT

Using the internet or your school library, find out more about astronomer Johannes Kepler and his laws of planetary motion. Write a two-page report and share it with your class.

The courtyard of Westminster Abbey, where Isaac Newton was buried after his death in 1725. Today a large monument there commemorates the great scientist.

WORDS TO UNDERSTAND

exchequer—the official British government account into which tax receipts and other public monies are paid.

sect—a philosophical, political, or religious group that is regarded as different from the mainstream.

theology—"The science of divine things," dealing with God, His nature and attributes, and His relations with man and the universe.

CHAPTER 6
A Very Eminent Citizen

Newton was forty-four years old when his *Principia* was published. His assistant and secretary, Humphrey Newton, remembered the intense concentration that went into writing it. (Despite their shared surname, Humphrey was not related to Isaac.) Newton seldom slept before two or three o'clock in the morning, and, when doing chemical experiments, not till five or six. He would start his work again after resting for only four or five hours. He would pace his room so restlessly that "you might have thought him to be educated at Athens among the Aristotelean **sect**" [it was Aristotle's custom to walk up and down while teaching at the Lyceum]. He often left untouched what food was prepared for him. On the rare occasions when he dined in the college hall, if not reminded he "would go very carelessly, with shoes down of heels, and his head scarcely combed."

Few people went to the small number of lectures Newton gave as Lucasian Professor. Sometimes he came back from an empty hall. Early in 1687 his work was interrupted when he went to London with the vice-chancellor and others from Cambridge University. King James II, a convert to Catholicism, had been on the throne for two years. Cambridge refused his order to give a degree to a Benedictine monk, and its officials were summoned to appear before a notorious judge, George Jeffreys. Jeffreys would not listen to their explanations, and the vice-chancellor was deprived of his offices. In November 1688 William of Orange landed in England and King James was forced into exile. The vice-chancellor was restored, and Newton served for a little over a year as the representative for Cambridge in Parliament called in 1689.

New Challenges

The work of composing the *Principia*, together with pressures in his personal and intellectual life, led to Newton's mental breakdown in 1693. He is said to have spoken only once during his year in Parliament, and then only to ask an usher to open a window. But he had influential friends, especially Charles Montague, a former student whose political star rose rapidly. His friends tried to get Newton a public post, at first without much success. During the same year, Newton went back to Grantham to nurse his mother devotedly during her last illness. Newton had again taken up his **theological** work, but tried to suppress a work challenging the orthodox view of the Holy Trinity that he had earlier been anxious to publish in Holland in translation without putting his name to it.

In 1693 his friends Samuel Pepys (famous for his diary) and philosopher John Locke were startled to receive strange letters from Newton. Pepys wrote at once to Cambridge to ask a friend to visit Newton. The letter had greatly disturbed him, "lest it should arise from that which of all mankind I should least dread from

SERIOUS SCHOLAR

Isaac Newton's assistant once wrote to a friend that he had heard Newton laugh only once when he was at Cambridge. That was when someone asked him what was the use of studying Euclid. But as Newton became internationally known for his scientific work, he became more friendly and cheerful. The assistant write that engaging in London society had changed Newton so that he was "easily made to smile, if not to laugh."

This portrait of Newton was painted around 1709, when the scientist was at the height of his fame.

Samuel Pepys (1633–1703), the famous diarist, a founding member of the Royal Society and a close friend of Newton.

him and most lament for." But Newton's recovery was rapid and his mental powers, soon tested in scientific controversies and new public duties, showed their old vigor.

Newton said goodbye to Cambridge in 1695 to take up the Wardenship of the Mint that Montague, now Chancellor of the **Exchequer**, managed to get for him. The post was no mere cushy job. Montague had decided to reissue all the coin of the realm. Widespread clipping of gold and silver coin had devalued English currency and become a scandal. Clipped coin was now called in, melted, and reissued with milled edges at the mint in London and at branches in several towns. Only first-class management made it possible to do the job in two years, in the midst of a war with France and with continuing hostility from the Parliamentary opposition. Although Montague's party was defeated at the next election, the Tories kept Newton on and made him Master of the Mint in 1699.

Newton had lost his Parliamentary seat during the election of 1690. He was reelected for Cambridge in 1701. Two years later he received the honor of being elected president of the Royal Society. He was reelected president every year for the remaining twenty-five years of his life.

While busy with the recoinage, Newton had written to the Royal Astronomer,

John Flamsteed, criticizing him for spreading the rumor that he, Newton, would soon offer an improved theory of the motion of the moon. He did not, he said, wish to be "teased by foreigners about mathematical things, or to be thought by our own people to be trifling away my time about them, when I should be about the King's business." But he had not turned away from science. In 1704 his *Opticks* was published. Contrasting with the highly technical and mathematical *Principia*, it long remained a popular work. Newton worked hard upon revisions for the second and third editions of the *Principia* that appeared in his lifetime, edited by younger mathematicians.

His encouragement of the talents of younger friends was one of his most attractive features. But there was plainly another side to his character. John Locke,

John Flamsteed (1646–1719) and Gottfried Wilhelm von Leibniz (1646–1716), two men who were targets of Newton's anger. Flamsteed, the royal astronomer, had annoyed Newton with his disagreements to such an extent that Newton took out of Flamsteed's control the publication of his life's work in astronomy. Leibniz was Newton's great rival to the claim to have discovered calculus.

The Secret to the Success of The Royal Society

Bill Bryson

Scan here to learn more about the Royal Society:

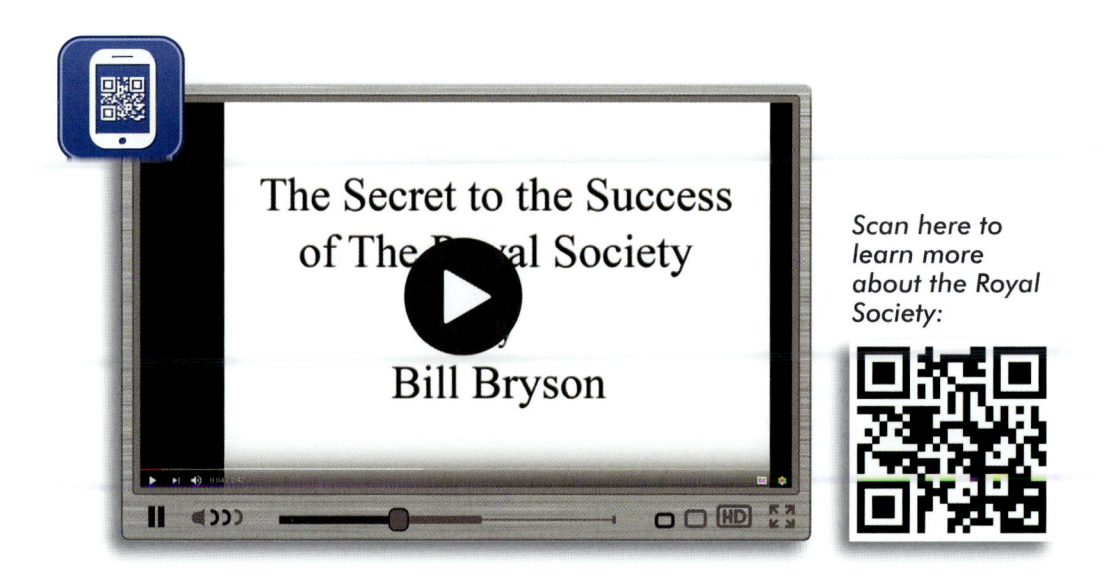

who greatly admired him, described Newton to a friend as "a little too apt to raise in himself suspicions where there is no ground." Flamsteed, a less impartial witness, called him "insidious, ambitious, and excessively covetous of praise, and impatient." Flamsteed had reason for his bitterness. When he angered Newton by disagreements, Newton had seen to it that Flamsteed would have no control over the printing of his life's work in astronomy. The great German philosopher and man of science, Leibniz, was another man who became the target of Newton's anger. Newton had once admitted that each of them had discovered calculus on their own at about the same time. Once a dispute on priority had been fanned by others, Newton masterminded a supposedly neutral committee that the Royal Society appointed at Leibniz's request. Leibniz's conduct in the affair was not blameless. But he was made to seem to have stolen his discovery from Newton.

Final Years

Carried in his extreme old age by coach or sedan chair to preside over meetings of the Royal Society, Newton outlived old enemies like Hooke, Flamsteed, and Leibniz. Even in the country of Descartes, leading younger philosophers like Voltaire wished to sweep the Cartesian vortices from the scientific skies to leave only the gravitational attraction and empty space of Newton. Locke and Newton became patron saints of the great movement of thought known as the Enlightenment. When the Romantic Movement rejected the ideals of that "Age of Reason" in the later eighteenth century, Newton inevitably became for them a symbol of a narrow and cold rationality. For the Romantics, deep feeling and a sense of mystery in life were more important in understanding the world than a mathematical analysis of its motions.

Neither Enlightenment nor Romantic image did full justice to the Newton whom the poet William Wordsworth imagined voyaging over "strange seas of thought." Like many other great innovators, he turned his face to the past even as he pointed the way forward. His religious roots lay in Protestant fundamentalism, which means he believed everything in the Bible to be true beyond doubt. The Biblical studies on which he worked for many years aimed to prove that the

THE IMPORTANCE OF NEWTON

For a long time it seemed that Newton's explanation of gravity might be the most important scientific discovery ever. The French physicist Pierre Laplace remarked in the late eighteenth century that Newton was the luckiest scientist who had ever lived, for there was only one system of scientific laws which explained the workings of the universe, and Newton had found it. However, since the early twentieth century there have been many new discoveries—including Albert Einstein's general theory of relativity—that have changed the way physicists understand gravity. But Newton's law still rules the way in which we analyze and predict the motion of physical objects in all kinds of circumstances.

prophetic books had foretold the course of ancient history in the most accurate detail. While eager in the defense of his scientific claims, he seriously thought about putting forward evidence in the second edition of the *Principia* to prove that the Law of Universal Gravitation was hidden in the ancient idea of the "music of the spheres," and that Pythagoras had solved that riddle. He felt at home in the world of the alchemist, and clung to a world of ideas which his own work was to do most to destroy, and to which the Romantics would seek to return.

Newton suffered ill health from about 1722. In 1725 he moved to Kensington from his home in Jermyn Street, Piccadilly, to breathe a purer country air. In February of that year he felt well enough to preside over a meeting of the Royal Society in town. His last illness soon followed. He sank into unconsciousness on March 18 and died early in the morning of March 20, being then in his eighty-fifth year. He was buried after a magnificent funeral in Westminster Abbey. "Let mortals rejoice," read the words upon the monument erected to him in 1731, "that there has existed such and so great an ornament of the human race."

Perfected by the work of eighteenth- and nineteenth-century scientists, Newton's system of the world appeared to be his permanent monument, until Albert Einstein made it a special case of a more comprehensive theory. Newton himself searched for a knowledge that went beyond any physical theory.

"I do not know," said Newton, "what I may appear to the world; but to myself I seem to have been only like a boy, playing on the seashore, and diverting myself in now and then finding a smoother pebble or a prettier shell than ordinary, while the great ocean of truth lay all undiscovered before me."

TEXT-DEPENDENT QUESTIONS

1. Why was Newton's work interrupted in 1687?
2. What government position did Newton take in 1695?
3. Where did Newton move to in 1725?

RESEARCH PROJECT

In the early twentieth century, German physicist Albert Einstein developed his theories of relativity, which improved upon Newton's laws of gravity in explaining how the universe works. Using your school library or the internet, do some research on Einstein and his Theory of Relativity. What are the differences between Newton's laws and Einstein's theory? Explain your findings in a two-page paper and share it with your class.

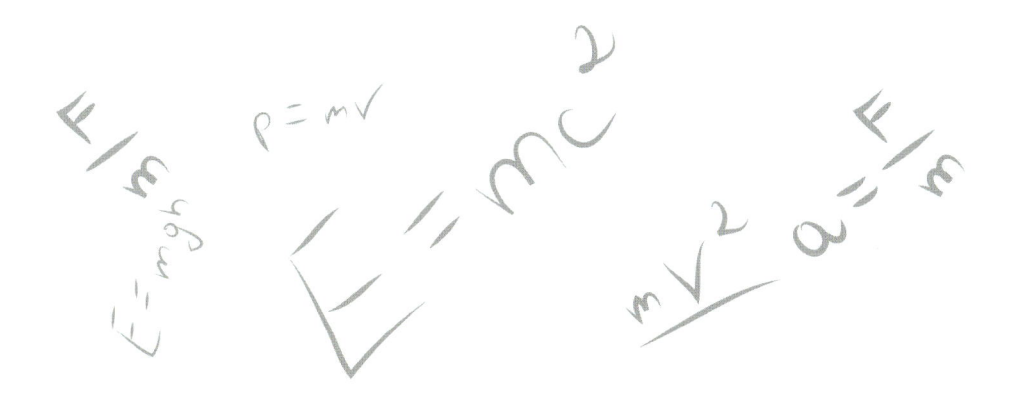

Chronology

1642
Born on Christmas Day at Woolsthorpe, Lincolnshire, England.

1654
Admitted to King's School, Grantham, and lodged with apothecary in town.

1656
Recalled from school on death of stepfather and return of mother to Woolsthorpe.

1660
Prepares for Cambridge at Grantham.

1661
Admitted sub-sizar at Trinity College, Cambridge.

1665
Bachelor of Arts. Plague causes return to Woolsthorpe, except for perhaps short visit in 1666.

1667
Return to Cambridge. Master of Arts.

1668
Elected senior fellow of Trinity College.

1669–71
Appointed Lucasian Professor of Mathematics to succeed Barrow.

1671
Sends reflecting telescope to Royal Society.

1672

Sends new theory of light and colors to Royal Society. Elected fellow of Royal Society.

1674

Permitted by royal patent to hold college fellowship without being ordained, while Lucasian Professor.

1676

Binomial Theorem sent to Royal Society.

1679

Letter from Hooke revives Newton's interest in mechanics.

1684

Halley's visit to Newton and promise of proof of inverse-square law for elliptical orbits.

1686

Printing of Book I of *Principia Mathematica Philosophia Naturalis* begun at Halley's expense.

1687

Books II and III reach the Royal Society in March and April; *Principia* appears in July.

1696

Appointed Warden of Royal Mint in London. Engaged in recoinage.

1699

Master of Mint.

1701

Finally resigns Lucasian Professorship.

1703
President of Royal Society.

1704
Opticks published.

1705
Knighted by Queen Anne at Cambridge.

1713
Royal Society committee reports on calculus priority dispute between Newton and Leibniz. Second edition of *Principia*.

1724
Moves from Piccadilly to village of Kensington.

1726
Third edition of *Principia* published.

1727
Newton dies and is buried in Westminster Abbey.

Further Reading

Chambers, John. *The Metaphysical World of Isaac Newton: Alchemy, Prophecy, and the Search for Lost Knowledge*. New York: Destiny Books, 2018.

Gleick, James. *Isaac Newton*. New York: Random House, 2003.

Iliffe, Rob. *Priest of Nature: The Religious Worlds of Isaac Newton*. New York: Oxford University Press, 2017.

Morus, Iwan Rhys. *The Oxford Illustrated History of Science*. New York: Oxford University Press, 2017.

Pascal, Janet B. *Who Was Isaac Newton?* New York: Grosset and Dunlap, 2014.

Steele, Philip. *Isaac Newton: The Scientist Who Changed Everything*. Washington, DC: National Geographic Books, 2013.

Wootton, David. *The Invention of Science: A New History of the Scientific Revolution*. New York: Harper Perennial, 2016.

Internet Resources

https://royalsociety.org

Website of the Royal Society, a fellowship of the world's most eminent scientists and the oldest scientific academy in continuous existence.

https://www.newton.ac.uk

The Isaac Newton Institute for Mathematical Sciences is an international visitor research institute. It runs research programs on selected themes in mathematics and the mathematical sciences, with applications over a wide range of science and technology.

https://www.sciencenewsforstudents.org

Science News for Students is an award-winning online publication dedicated to providing age-appropriate, topical science news to learners, parents and educators.

http://www.pbs.org/wgbh/nova

The website of NOVA, a science series that airs on PBS. The series produces in-depth science programming on a variety of topics, from the latest breakthroughs in technology to the deepest mysteries of the natural world.

https://www.physics.org

This website from the Institute of Physics is intended to provide resources about physics to students of all ages.

Series Glossary of Key Terms

anomaly—something that differs from the expectations generated by an established scientific idea. Anomalous observations may inspire scientists to reconsider, modify, or come up with alternatives to an accepted theory or hypothesis.

evidence—test results and/or observations that may either help support or help refute a scientific idea. In general, raw data are considered evidence only once they have been interpreted in a way that reflects on the accuracy of a scientific idea.

experiment—a scientific test that involves manipulating some factor or factors in a system in order to see how those changes affect the outcome or behavior of the system.

hypothesis—a proposed explanation for a fairly narrow set of phenomena, usually based on prior experience, scientific background knowledge, preliminary observations, and logic.

natural world—all the components of the physical universe, as well as the natural forces at work on those things.

objective—to consider and represent facts without being influenced by biases, opinions, or emotions. Scientists strive to be objective, not subjective, in their reasoning about scientific issues.

observe—to note, record, or attend to a result, occurrence, or phenomenon.

science—knowledge of the natural world, as well as the process through which that knowledge is built through testing ideas with evidence gathered from the natural world.

subjective—referring to something that is influenced by biases, opinions, and/or emotions. Scientists strive to be objective, not subjective, in their reasoning about scientific issues.

test—an observation or experiment that could provide evidence regarding the accuracy of a scientific idea. Testing involves figuring out what one would expect to observe if an idea were correct and comparing that expectation to what one actually observes.

theory—a broad, natural explanation for a wide range of phenomena in science. Theories are concise, coherent, systematic, predictive, and broadly applicable, often integrating and generalizing many hypotheses. Theories accepted by the scientific community are generally strongly supported by many different lines of evidence. However, theories may be modified or overturned as new evidence is discovered.

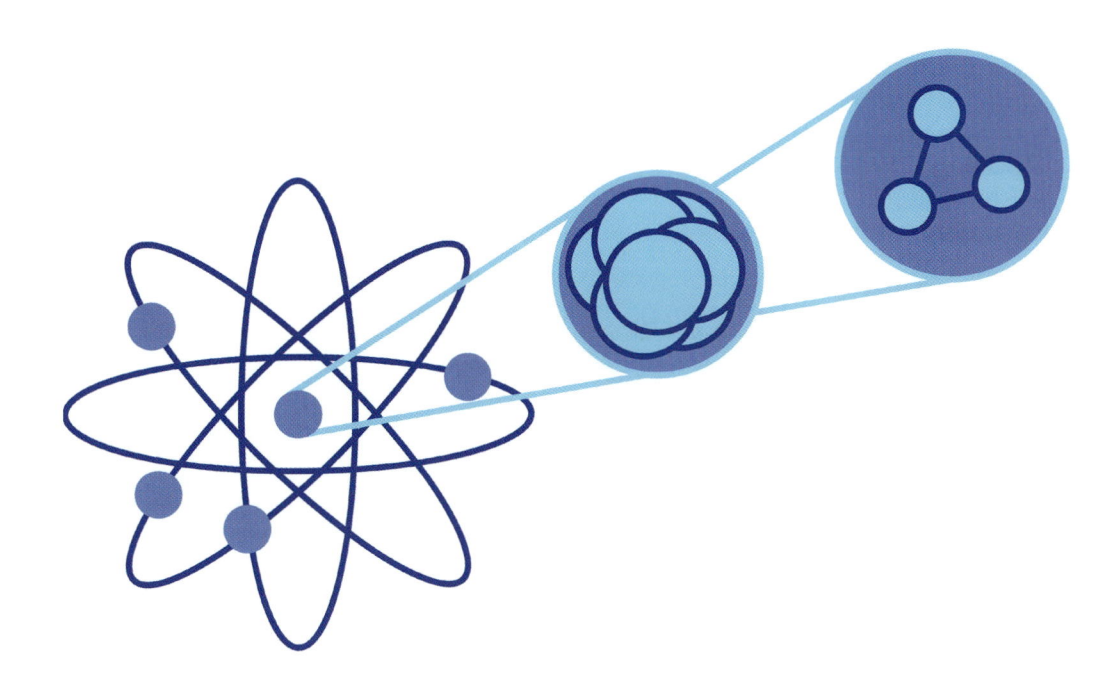

Index

A

ab Hohenheim, Philippus (Paracelsus), 36, 37, 39, 40
aberration, 44
acceleration, 45, 63
Age of Reason, 83
air, 23
alchemical studies, 66
alchemist, 39–40, 41, 84
alchemy, 6, 8
alembic, 30, 40
Alighieri, Dante, 17
Almagest (Ptolemy), 21
Anglican church, 11
apothecary, 6, 10
Aquinas, St. Thomas, 28
Aristarchus (Samos), 19, 21
Aristotle
    air, study of, 31–32
    alternative thinking, 39–40, 44, 65
        importance of, 20–21, 23–24, 25, 26, 38–39
        scientific beliefs, 14, 17, 18, 19
Assyrians, 26
Astronomia Nova (New Astronomy), 63
astronomy, 39
atmosphere, 72
atomism, 19, 20
attractive force, 65, 67
automaton, 35

B

Bacon, Francis, 17, 22
barometer, 30, 32
Barrow, Isaac, 46, 47, 51
Boyle, Robert, 42, 43, 66–67

C

calculus, 6, 7
Cambridge Platonists, 69
Cambridge Univeristy (London), 7, 13–14, 16, 46–47, 53, 77
Cartesian vortices, 62, 67, 69, 72, 83
Catholicism, 77
Cavaliers (Royalists), 11, 12, 13
celestial mechanism, 60
celestial spheres, 21
cell, 67
centrifugal force, 58, 62, 65
centripetal force, 58, 70
Charles I, King, 11, 12
Charles II, King, 11, 43, 49, 77
Charles, Montague, 78, 80
chemical studies, 66
Christian (Kingdom), 28
chromatic aberration, 47, 53, 56
circular motion, 62, 65
coin, 80
color, theory of, 53
Commonwealth, 11, 13
concave, 16, 20
convex, 44, 56
Copernicus, Nicolas, 18, 26, 27, 30, 39, 50
cosmology, 16, 18
Council of the Holy office, 30
Cromwell, Oliver, 11
Crusades (Middle East), 28

D

de Roberval, Gilles Personne, 65
Democritus, 19
Descartes, René
    New Science, 18, 35–36, 49–50, 53
    physical theories, 33, 34, 38–39
    as a recent thinker, 14
Dialogo (Galileo), 30
differential calculus, 45–46
discoveries of Newton
    calculus, 6, 7
    laws of Universal Gravitation, 7, 46, 59, 65, 84
    white light, 7
Dolland, 56
don, 13
Donne, John, 39
downward motion, 62

E

Earl of Cork, 43
Early Greek thinkers, 23
Earth, 19, 23–24, 25, 26, 27, 35
Egyptians, 26

Tyson, Neil DeGrasse, 56 (QR code)

U
uniform acceleration, 70
uniform circular motion, 60
universal gravitation, 59, 65, 84

V
velocity, 45, 70
Venus, 21
Voltaire, François-Marie Arouet, 83
von Leibniz, Gottfried Wilhelm, 81

W
Wardenship of the Mint, 80
water, 23
wave motion, 72
weight, 69
Westminster Abbey, 76, 84
Wilkins, John, 66–67
William of Orange, 77
Woolsthrope (England), 7, 9, 11
Wordsworth, William, 83
Wren, Christopher, 43, 65, 66

About the Author

Paul M. Nittany was born in Kenya, and currently lives in New York City. A graduate of Columbia University, he has written on science and society in seventeenth century England, and is currently working on a study of Newton's alchemical manuscripts.

Photo Credits

Library of Congress: 47, 71; National Aeronautics and Space Administration: 68 (bottom); National Portrait Gallery, London: 1; used under license from Shutterstock, Inc.: 9, 19, 22, 46, 58; Martin Charles Hatch / shutterstock.com: 16; Brendan Howard / shutterstock.com: 34; PlusONE / shutterstock.com: 48; Natalya Okorokova / shutterstock.com: 76; Wellcome Library: 6, 8, 10, 12, 25, 26, 27, 30, 33, 37, 41, 43, 52, 55, 61, 63, 64, 68 (top), 72, 79, 80, 81.